Riya Anne Polcastro

The Truth about Cows:

a Polcastro Reader

Also by Polcastro:

Jane.
Suicide in Tiny Increments
The Last Magdalene
The Left Behind Trilogy —
Book One: The Forbidden Voyage
Book Two: Brave New Planet

coming soon —
Left Behind Book Three
Teeth (working title)

Thanks for choosing *The Truth about Cows: A Polcastro Reader*! Reviews are much appreciated. And if you want to pass it on to a friend, or ten, that's cool too.

Contents

Blasts from the Past—memoir en pedacitas

One Year—One Lie—Forever More in Generoso, MX

It was a lie and your mother knew it but she didn't stop him. She tried to take herself out of the equation with a bottle of tequila instead, but her liver was too strong for the poison.

It was only for a year. That's what he said as he scouted retired ice cream trucks and delivery vans. It was only for a year, but none of those would do—they simply were not large enough, or fit enough, to make the long haul. "It's only for a year," he said, when he pulled up in an old yellow school bus. He promised, over and over, while pulling out row after row of green vinyl bench seats. "You won't even have time to miss your friends."

A year is a long time when you're six. A year might as well be a decade.

But you don't sell most of what you own at weekly garage sales if you'll only be gone for a year. You don't watch your mother sort through decades of personal belongings, stowing years of keepsakes and mementos inside a yellow school bus. You don't hear her talking about how she packed the handmade velvet dress she's saving for your future daughter onto that same bus. Not if you're coming back. Not if it will only be a year.

For a year, you rent a storage unit. For a year, you get a neighbor to watch your house—you don't sell it. But the realtor came and staked her claim with a brand new sign in the front yard right next to your favorite climbing tree anyway. For a year, you pack up the family station wagon and lease a furnished apartment—you don't drive a giant yellow bus with the word "school" blacked out, stuffed with couches and tables, a washer and dryer, what's left of your earthly possessions, across the Mexican border.

You might sound a little bitter right now, but you're not. You don't resent your father for never wanting to come back. You don't resent him for his lies, or your mother for going along with them. Because . . . because, in a way, it was the greatest time of your life. Even now, grown as you are, with children of your own, it is still a big part of who you are. Maybe you even find yourself wishing you could give them the same experience. Not the deceit or enabling, but the life experience of a world beyond their coddled American existence.

Maybe you've done everything you can not to spoil them, to explain what most of the world is like, but you know that is nothing like seeing it with their own two eyes. Smelling it. Touching it. Living it. They don't know what it's like to shit in an outhouse. A real one—not some pansy ass Honey Bucket—but a hole dug in the ground, already half full with human waste, and stinking so bad that they have to hold their breath in the hundred and ten degree weather. Your daughter, she's not much bigger than you were the first time your parents took you to the colonias—the first time you teetered on the edge of that seat made of plywood, scared to death of falling in, your mother holding you by your pits. Your son, he's already five years older than you were the last time you sat so confidently, your butt finally big enough to cover most of the hole and assuage your fear of drowning in a soup of pee and poop. But the way he is already so entrenched in this artificial lifestyle you know he'd hold it to the point of infection, or at least get bitten by a rattlesnake while pissing in the tumbleweeds, before he'd open that wooden door with the moon cut out.

Your kids, neither of them have ever seen a man dying slow at home, his family doing their best to keep him comfortable despite his broken bones and his body slowly turning septic. They've never watched hands laid and miracles prayed for, a thin veil over the ulterior motives of a white American lead Evangelical movement proselytizing its way through this Catholic nation by way of womanizing missionaries. They've never seen the settlements built in desperate poverty—the colonias hidden in the mountains—hundreds of one room shacks made of spare plywood and cardboard, many home to three, sometimes four generations.

But neither have they seen what it is like to truly give it away.

Your kids, they've never stared generosity in its beaming, sun worn face. They've never been given the shirt off of a stranger's back. They've never been the guest of honor sitting on a floor made of packed dirt and bottle caps, a bowl of fresh, homemade menudo in their lap. They couldn't even fathom what a feat this caldo is, accomplished without running water or electricity, let alone a refrigerator. Maybe, even as an adult, you have a hard time understanding why a mother of six would use her one day off travelling to the city, hauling back fresh ingredients packed in ice, only to wash those ingredients with water she had to carry from the communal pila and cook over a camp stove, all just to feed you and your family a hot meal. Your family that lived in a comfortable three bedroom cement house on a paved road with indoor plumbing and a personal pila as a backup for when the city supply ran dry.

You could call it culture shock—when those in the most need are the first to give. But you'd have to admit that it is only now that the shock is settling in. Settling in between you and your offspring. Of course, it's not their fault. Your son, your daughter, they're also products of the society they've been brought up in; one where all of the forces around them are destined to be stronger than the lessons of your childhood. What they need, you know, are lessons of their own. So you take out a map and start to ponder.

Where could you take them, where could they see what life is really about—just for a year? Just one year. Or maybe two. But you know better. You know that given the choice, you might not come back either.

One Year – One Lie – Forever More in Generoso, MX first appeared in the Spring 2015 issue of Dirty Chai Magazine.

An Illegal in Mexico

I don't know how it is now, but back when teased hair could be found west of Texas and a young, not yet bankrupt MC Hammer bragged that no one could touch him, Tecate was a city where you could rent the discarded shell of a mansion for a few hundred dollars a month. It was too high a price for the average local family and most of these places were gobbled up by expatriates instead. Paupers back home; here we could live like kings.

The big cement house at the top of the hill was different. The people that moved in there didn't have blond hair or blue eyes. They didn't send their children to private school on the other side of the border. They were monolingual, but in the national tongue, not English, and they bought their sundries with pesos, not dollars.

They also did not waste their money remodeling and painting and adorning the unfinished mansion. Even after they moved in the giant house continued to hide in plain sight; camouflaged by the monochrome gray that covered its every inch, from the four foot wall that surrounded the property, to the flat roof that stood almost invisible above the skyline.

A girl named Beatriz lived in that big gray shell. She was in second grade and I was in fourth but she towered over me. Her hair was kinky and her lips full but I didn't know anything about race back then. Every day after school we met in front of my house and lied to my mother about her parents being home. Then we would skip up the hill where, more often than not, we would have the giant empty place to ourselves.

Inside, the mansion was just as gray as the outside. The walls, the floors, the winding staircase; all made from the same bare cement. All of that gray was like a clean slate for our imaginations, a blank canvas for whatever game or drama we could envision. There was a room to suit our every purpose: a bedroom with a wall of mirrors where we perfected our Running Man; a parlor where I pretended to pour drinks from behind the bar and Beatriz puffed on a pen like a siren from an old black and white film; a living room with a spooky fireplace that moaned through our ghost stories; bedrooms that could only be reached from the second floor balcony made the perfect hotel for our travels as international superstars. We sauntered down the curve of the staircase, debutants making our grand entrance to the ball. We pulled the lid off the pila and leaned in to scoop buckets of water out of the underground tank for water fights. We chased each other with naïve giddiness, just a stumble's length away from the uncovered hole.

It was hot almost the whole year round. Summer was the only real season. Even in the dead of January I don't remember the afternoon temperatures ever dropping below sixty. Once there was a patch of frost on the ground, we tried to have a snowball fight, that didn't work out so well. Where there was no winter, there was even less spring. It rained hard for a few days. That was it, that was spring, and it was hot as ever again. But we didn't mind, we got to eat a lot of ice cream and make popsicles by filling plastic bags with juice and freezing them. And we loved fetching water from the pila and jumping into homemade brick swimming pools unencumbered by filtration systems and bleach. Even on August days when the rot of dead dog simmered in the dirt field we used as a short cut to the tortilla factory, I never yearned for fall. I never wished for a breeze to cool the baking outhouses in the colonias when we delivered beans and rice with Dad. I never even thought to. Autumn was an abstract concept. Something we learned in school but didn't see in real life unless you count a few clouds and a remote thunderstorm or two. The sun turned my hair as yellow as straw and my skin a caramel I would chase through hundreds of tanning beds as an adult back in Oregon. But if it changed the leaves on the palm trees or littered them across the streets it was never enough for me to notice. And it certainly never did anything about the puddles of heat that shimmered in waves across the road. Or the cockcroaches. Or the giant red ants that would bite us on the ass if we squatted in the dirt for too long.

When school started back up in September it was a hundred and something. All of us girls at the private Christian school on the California border were nonetheless cursed with the shin length dresses required by the institution's cult like obsession with gender. So much for sports, right? Except we still annihilated the boys in kickball games. We still climbed the monkey bars and fought on the playground.

Our homesick teachers decorated their classrooms in the oranges, yellows, and reds of leaves falling and gourds ripening and planned home visits to meet our families. It was a sneaky move to assess our godliness, to spy for rosaries and statues of the Virgin Mary. To determine who lived up to their definition of Christianity, and who had failed to convert.

Attending Tecate Christian School also came with the expectation that we abandon Spanish at the border. Every morning we crossed, either on foot or in the family delivery van. The other kids would show their passports, their papeles. My brother and I would declare "American" and be waved through. Going back wasn't much different, we still didn't have papers.

Fast Feels—for the literary heart

A Boy's Best Friend

The orange is a find for sure. Its skin is still intact, no
smooshes or dents, no gashes or mold. Sammy rips into
the treasure, oblivious to the mud stains on his chubby
little hands. Citrus squirts and runs out of the fruit,
collecting in the dimples on the back of his knuckles and
the spaces between his fingers. He laps the muddy juice
up before it can dry. Pieces of peel fall to the ground and
Boshka rushes from her hiding place under the very last
step in the stairwell to investigate. Her whiskers twitch at
the zest and she retreats to the boy's side. She nuzzles her
head against him, rubs the length of her body, little pink
nose to the tip of her black and gray striped tail, against
him in that special way that cats do. Sammy ignores her
and tears the orange in two. He shoves the first segment
past his greedy lips. Half of it juts out, more fruit than
there is room in his tiny mouth. His molars work to break
down the flesh and juice trickles from the corners of his
mouth.

"Meow," Boshka says, rubbing her head against his
other side. But Sammy can't stop to pat her head or reach
for the fish he found for her dinner. His vacant stomach
aches and churns with unused acid. It isn't possible to
chew fast enough. Boshka nuzzles the crown of her head
against the pocket of his unwashed jeans, impatient.
"Meeooooww!" She can smell the fish, about to turn, and
her belly rumbles. She needs it. She needs that piece of
fish. Now!

"Leave me alone," the boy whines as he elbows the cat
not so gently in the ribs. He feels horrible the second he

does it. Racked with guilt, he sets what is left of the orange down on the cement, stands, and reaches into his pocket for two slabs of pink flesh which he lays down in front of Boshka. Boshka always fares better than the boy. When there is nothing for him to scavenge, the cat can at least kill a mouse or a bird, or jump into the dumpster outside of McDonald's.

Sammy squats back down and picks up his orange. He dusts the grit and grime off the bottom the best he can and tears another segment off. Of course it will not be enough. When he crawls into his sleeping bag under the stairs and closes his eyes and tries to sleep his tummy will still roar and his tears will still fall and the cat will wipe them away with her tongue covered in sandpaper and he will be glad that even though all of his four years are a blur and he does not remember what his family looked like, at least Boshka is still with him.

No Purchase Necessary

It all started when I was a kid. I saw it on a cereal box: no purchase necessary. I asked Mama what it meant and she said people could enter the contest without buying the cereal. Mama would never buy the cereal. It was not on the list.

Eggs
Milk
Bacon
Spaghetti Noodles
Spaghetti Sauce
Potatoes
Apples
Bananas
Onions

Those things were on the list. Cereal was not.

I asked Mama can I enter the contest but she said we did not have time for that. We had to get the shopping done and get home in time to make dinner for Papa.

I didn't understand. My bottom lip quivered. I tried to hide it by scrunching up my face. I cried anyway. No purchase necessary!

She bent down and plucked the box from the shelf. She showed me the side of the box. She said I know Mathew sweetie. But we have to write this address down and send them a postcard and we don't have time for that. We have to hurry.

I stared at the rules on the side of the box. I stared until Mama put it back on the shelf and tugged me down the aisle. When we got home, I found a postcard in Papa's desk and wrote the address from the rules on it:

555 W 1st St. Suite 123
New York, NY 10016

I put the post card in the mailbox and waited for my prize. The mail lady came every day between one and two thirty, except Saturday and Sunday. On Saturday it was a man. He did not like it when I talked to him while he put the mail in the boxes. On Sunday no one came and there was no mail. The mail lady did not mind if I talked to her. She laughed at my jokes.

Why did the frog cross the road?

Because he wanted to croak.

The mail lady was very nice. But she never brought my prize from the cereal contest.

Now that I am almost grown up I know why. I know a lot more than when I was a kid. I know you have to put stamps on postcards or else they don't go anywhere. I learned all about stamps from Teacher. Teacher says I shouldn't call her that. She has a name. But when I look at her face I can't remember what it is. Jenny or Sarah. Or maybe Amy. She says she is not a teacher. She is a life skills coach. Teacher is easier to say and it makes more sense because she teaches me stuff. Like how to write grocery lists and use my bank card at the store. And take the bus to work. Grownups don't get rides from their parents. She teaches me all of the things I have to learn before I can move out of Mama and Papa's. Things like you have to put a stamp on postcards if you want them to go to the address you write on the back. Now I know I never had a chance at that contest. My postcard never made it there. The mail lady threw it away.

Today Teacher is going to help me write a real grocery list and then she is taking me to the store to buy all of the stuff on it. I make sure cereal is the first thing on my list. She tells me that they will probably have cereal at the group home and I don't need to buy my own. I just smile and nod. Sometimes grownups don't understand. I hope I'm not like that when I grow up.

When we get to the store, Teacher reminds me only the stuff on your list. Just like Mama. Teacher is only a few years older than me but she knows so much. Like where to find the bananas. And the animal crackers. And my favorite fruit snacks. I can't imagine doing this alone. All by myself with so many aisles and so many boxes and jars and cans. She tells me not to worry. She says we'll practice lots.

When we get to the checkout Teacher asks me why I didn't pick out any cereal. I looked at lots of boxes but I put all of them back on the shelf. I tell her no purchase necessary. She makes a face at my answer but I don't know what she means by it through all the swirling. I wiggle trying to shake off her stare. Then she asks me what does no purchase necessary mean and I am really happy because finally I know about something and Teacher does not. I tell her about how I can enter the contests without buying the cereal. But she isn't surprised or excited. She just says so that's why you wanted to look at cereal?

There are so many prizes! Jet skis. MP3 players. Trips to Disneyland. I don't understand why everyone doesn't spend more time in the cereal aisle. I don't think Teacher believes me about the contests but I'll show her when I win.

There are lots of postcards in Papa's desk. Stamps too. I take them up to my room and write out the addresses one by one. Just like they look in my head. Next I write my own address in one corner and put a stamp in the other corner like Teacher showed me. After dinner I walk to the big blue mailbox next to the store where Papa buys big boxes of beer. When I get home he is yelling something about where did his stamps go. I go to my room so that he won't know it was me.

Teacher says they are looking for a new home for me now. She says I am ready to move out of Mama and Papa's. She says I'll make lots of new friends.

It will be weird not to live with Mama and Papa but I don't think they want me anymore. I heard Mama say she was tired of taking care of me. Papa said it was their turn. My eyes watered and it got tough to breathe.

The first house is blue. A dog barks when Teacher knocks. It is a sharp, high pitched bark. I stick my thumbs in my ears to block it out. A woman comes to the door. She is old. Her hair is blue. The skin on her hands drips with wrinkles. She tells us her name but it swirls back into her face before I can hear it. She says to follow her. She stops at every room and tells us about it. This is the sitting room. This is the wash room. This is the dining room. This is the kitchen. There is someone in the kitchen. His tongue is thick and slow. It is still hanging out of his mouth when his name gets caught in the whirlwind of his face.

The old woman with the blue hair and drippy skin leads us down a hall. She shows us the bedrooms. In one room there is a half-bald man. His glasses are an inch thick. He sits on the bed and stares at nothing and mumbles. He mumbles from the moment the old woman opens the door to the moment she closes it. He mumbles through his name. He mumbles through mine. He mumbles through the wall after we have gone. She says the next room will be mine. She says it isn't much. She says it's just a bed and a desk but I can bring my own stuff.

My head shakes almost on its own. The mumbles scare me. Teacher's voice twirls through my head. I scream. I don't mean to. It just happens. It is loud. High pitched. My face gets red and hot. I run to Teacher's big white van.

I check the mail every day and wonder what went wrong. I sent off eight whole postcards and they all had a stamp and my address in the right corners. I should have won something by now. Teacher doesn't take me to see any more houses.

They were talking about me again. About how I am never going to leave. I run to my room. The water rushes out of my eyes. I grab my backpack and fill it with the important stuff. Like my baseball cards and video games. They want me gone, well I'll show them. I pound my way out of the house. The front door slams.

I am all the way across the street when the mail lady calls me back. She says she has a package for me. I don't think she is the same mail lady from when I was a kid but she is nice anyway. There is a big orange envelope in her hand. I can't move at first. My feet are stuck to the cement. She says she wonders what could be in it. I wonder too. When my feet unstick they force me to run back across the street.

She says be careful, you forgot to look for cars.

I don't take my eyes off the envelope. It is too small to be jet skis. I was sure I was going to win the jet skis. I tear at the thick orange envelope. The mail lady tells me I am littering. She bends over and tries to catch the orange strips as they fly away in the wind. My heart beats wild and fast. My hands shake. Something like a magazine slides out. The cover is slick and glossy. It is bright with lots of color. There is a small piece of paper attached to the front. I try to sound out the words on the page. Co… Co…Con…

The mail lady offers to help me. She has helped me read before. Congratulations. You are a runner up in our Disneyland Dream Vacation contest. We are pleased to award you with a one year subscription to Disney Magazine.

I stare at the magazine. I won?

She says you won!

Teacher takes me to the store again. This time I memorize fourteen addresses in the cereal aisle.

She doesn't believe me that I won so I show her the magazine in my back pocket. I tell her I was going to run away but then this magazine came. She says maybe we should start looking for a new home again but I want to stay at Mama and Papa's so I can keep getting the magazine.

A couple of days later Papa is yelling that his stamps are missing again. He pounds on my bedroom door. I'm scared so I go to the corner to hide. He calls my name. He yells boy are you in there?

The doorknob turns. The door creaks open. I watch it all frozen in my corner.

Boy why don't you answer me? Papa's big body eats up the doorway.

I ask Teacher if she can get my magazine from Mama and Papa's every month so I can still read it after I move. She asks me what I mean. Sometimes Teacher is confusing. Most grownups are. I don't know what to say so I stare at the ground. She tells me Mama and Papa will visit me. They can bring me the magazine.

I don't want Papa to visit me.

She says that we can change the address. Have the magazine go to my new group home instead. She asks if I am ready to look at another place.

A different place? Without the mumbles?

A different place. Without the mumbles.

Promise?

Promise.

Teacher finds me a new home. It is big and yellow and perfect. Yellow is my favorite color. Yellow is soft and nice. Yellow is never mean. Yellow never yells or screams.

It is a big yellow house with lots of empty rooms. Someday there will be other people in those rooms. People like me that are new to being grownups and have to move out of their Mamas' and Papas' houses too. But for now it's just me. Teacher tells me I'll get to adjust in peace. I don't know what that means but I like my new family.

My new Mama tells me what to call her. It disappears into her face. Same with my new Papa. In this family I have a brother. I never had a brother before. My brother's face doesn't swirl in on itself as fast as others' do. He is easier to look at, with his yellow hair and soft blue eyes.

Eyes are the hardest part. Most people I can't look at their eyes at all. Most people I'm lucky if I can even look at their noses. Faces make me dizzy. Names sound like nothingness. Like dead air swallowed by their whirlwind mouth.

Brother tells me not to call him Brother. He reminds me over and over of his name. In the kitchen when he says hello, Teacher says I must always say hello back so I say hello Brother.

My name…

Ok, Brother.

He laughs but I am not scared. I laugh too. In the living room he asks can he see the remote.

Yes Brother.

My name isn't Brother…

Of course it is. But then at dinner something changes. I hear it. I remember it. I say it.

Pass the potatoes.

Ok Ian.

There are smiles around the table. My new Mama and Papa look proud.

After dinner Ian comes into my room. He plops down next to me on the twin bed. He is close and warm but I don't recoil. We look at baseball cards. It is nice. Like having a friend.

He says you know I'm not really your brother right.

I'm not really sure what he means. Did he change his mind? Maybe he doesn't want to be my friend anymore. My chin trembles. I want to run away again but it is my room.

The next day Ian plops down on my bed again. He asks what'cha doing?

It is Saturday. I am doing what I do every Saturday.

He asks can he see and he leans his chin on my shoulder and I shudder a little. I'm not used to people touching me.

I mumble something and focus all of my attention on the last postcard. I write the To address as neat as possible. So that it will get there. I write the From address just as neat. So the mail lady will know where to bring my prize.

He asks again, can I see? I don't know if I should let him. But he smiles and when I look at his blue eyes his face does not swirl. Please?

I reach my hand out a couple of inches. My stomach is squishy and hollow. I say be careful.

He flips through them. Shuffles them. I wince. He asks what they are for.

I answer slowly contests.

He shuffles them again. He asks what kind of contests? Are these cereal companies?

I say no purchase necessary. Quiet. Almost a whisper.

He is quiet and my stomach gets squishier and squishier. His face starts to swirl but then he smiles and his voice is bright like the sunshine and he asks can you enter more than once?

I don't know what he means so I don't say anything at all.

Teacher doesn't come around very much anymore. I miss her. I'm still too scared to go to the store without her. What if she is mad at me? I thought she wanted me to move in with my new family.

It's Saturday again. Ian comes back into my room. Plops down on my bed. He has a stack of postcards. I look at him. Look at the postcards. Look back at him. He says the more you send in, the better chance you have of winning. Maybe he's right. I haven't won anything since the magazine.

But then I do! I do win! After Ian helps with all of the extra postcards I finally win again! It's a box like one that shoes come in. Ian brings it in from the mail. He brings it in to the living room where my first Mama is visiting. His big blue eyes sparkle and his voice is bright like the sunshine again. He hands me the box covered in brown paper. He says go ahead open it!

My first Mama asks what is that Mathew. She asks what did you win.

I don't answer because I don't know. I don't remember entering a shoe contest. I rip the paper off and it is a cardboard box with a lid just like a shoebox. But it isn't shoes. It is a bunch of stuff. I pull out something flat and smooth, something rolled up, an envelope. Ian yells out with each thing. A magnet! A calendar! Stickers! He says dude you won a swag box!

The word he says is new and weird. I don't know what it means. So all I hear is that I won a box. A box?

After my first Mama leaves I sit on my bed with the box I won. It is full of things with cartoons and words like Cheerios, Wheaties, Cinnamon Toast Crunch. There is a keychain. A bracelet. A plastic watch.

Ian jumps on my bed again. He says how cool it is that I won.

The corners of my lips tug up. That happens sometimes and it feels weird.

Ian digs into the box. He pulls out a small stuffed bee. He leans over the box. He asks do you think you won because of my extra postcards.

Maybe but I don't know so I don't say anything. His blue eyes get closer. So do his lips. Then his lips are on mine. And it isn't anything like when Marsha Hinsberg slobbered all over my face in the third grade and I had to see a special doctor for a month.

It is soft. Tingly. Not swirly at all.

It is safe like no purchase necessary.

Senya Says

Senya says there isn't any sense in waiting around for someone else to sweep you off your feet. Senya says sometimes you just have to make romance for yourself. Couples may have the monopoly, but they do not own the patent. Romance does not have to be chocolate covered strawberries and rose petals strewn across the bed. It is not just moonlit walks arm in arm, or a candlelit dinner for two. It in no way requires cards or stuffed teddy bears on Valentine's Day. It is about enjoying the uniqueness of the moment. It is stopping to smell the tulips and soak in the stars. It can be found anywhere and it can be just as good solo. No one needs a lover to experience life's beautiful moments.

Senya proposes a broader definition of romance, one that does not exclude singletons or those with prosaic partners, one that is so much more than the popular dichotomy allows, where romance can be the early morning fog in your own backyard or the sound of crickets at night. It can be as simple as using the good sheets and the expensive perfume; as modest as delighting in everyday life, relishing the beauty in the mundane. It can be the coffee and silence you savor before the rest of the house wakes. It can be a walk downtown or a drive through the countryside. For me, it is the ferry to Victoria, the potholes in Sooke, the sunset over English Bay, Stanley Park on a crisp summer morning. It is sitting on a wooden deck next to Lost Lagoon while swans float by, a turtle stretches out on a rock, raccoons beg for food. It is twilight in Vancouver, when the sun ducks behind the high-rises, the purple blue sky, the strips of pink on the edge of the skyline, the vibrations of youth and energy in the air. It is an afternoon retracing my steps along the cobblestones of Gastown, the lights and opulence of Coal Harbor after dark, mussels for one on False Creek. Romance is all the places where I can just be, where I can take it all in. On top of Spencer's Butte when the clouds are low. Sitting by a fire next to the McKenzie River. Standing behind waterfalls and wading across creeks. It is meandering through the capitol mall, Oregon in springtime, under ivy and cherry blossoms. It is getting up early enough to see the sunrise and hear the birds chirp. It is a walk on the beach. The winter sun, the crashing waves, the mist over the water, it is all still there even without someone to hold my hand. It is the smell of fallen apples, of grape vines. It is the riverfront lights twinkling in the water, coasting down the promenade on a cruiser. It is a bottle of red wine and gourmet cheese shared with friends. It is a fancy dinner without distractions, permission to be enchanted by cuisine and ambiance.

There is no reason a trip to Alaska should wait on a lover. Polar bears and beluga whales will not be around forever, let the glaciers romance you before they melt into the ocean. Visit the orcas around the Strait. Meet artists with home galleries and eat at bistros that only serve dinner from five to seven. Find hidden coves and the skeletons of old buildings sinking into the marsh. Trek through the Petrified Forest and across the lava beds of Bend. Rent a secluded cabin next to a hot spring. Whatever you choose, the point is to never sell yourself short on romance just because you don't have someone to share it with.

There is something about distance, something about getting away that makes everything a little more romantic, even if it is only for a few days, only a few hundred miles away. You can learn a lot about yourself on holiday alone, things you never knew or had forgotten: strengths, challenges, quirks. Fall in love with you all over again. Spoil yourself. Rent a room at the Sheraton, order room service, and a good wine. Dress up. Go to the theater or the opera. Splurge on a Town Car.

Much of what we consider romance is novel. Novel experiences and places. But if we sit around waiting for someone else to whisk us off to somewhere new, we may never experience those places. Don't miss out on Paris for a lover that will never get away from the office or Bora Bora just because you are single. Go by yourself, go with friends, make memories, take pictures, enjoy the moments while you have them. Make your own definition.

If love makes colors brighter, food taste better, life richer, why shouldn't it apply to everyone? Too many of us are living in black and white. We go through life waiting for someone else to make the grass green, the sky blue. Why? When we have the power to do it for ourselves? Still we do not understand how. We cannot imagine a holiday alone in anything more than drab shades of gray. And when we stroll through the park we do not see the tender shoots of grass draped in mist, we do not hear the baby birds chirp or the squirrels chatter. Attitude is everything. We have to commit to the now in the same way we would if we were with a lover. Push the thoughts from our heads, especially the negative ones. Pace is key. Go slow. Stop to admire the way the sun shines under a bridge. Don't rush past the spider web dusted in dew. Notice how it sparkles, how it reflects life. Take it all in: the fresh air, the ripple of a brook, the clouds that paint the sky.

Romance is that simple. Broken down to its most basic element, all it is, is slowing down enough to admire the magnificence of life. That is what couples do as they wander through botanical gardens and cuddle on the beach at sunset. They slow down enough to experience the sights, the sounds, the smells. It is as simple as that.

But what about that tingle in your soul, the butterflies

in your belly? Just because your love affair with yourself does not include the chemistry of sex it is not diminished any. You can still woo YOU with excitement and mystery. All of the beauty in life is still there, all of the sights and sounds and smells that make romance, they are there whether someone else has their arm around you or not.

Think back to childhood, back to sense memories. The warmth of the backyard sun on your face. The aroma of pears and plums ripening on the trees. The earthy green of tomato vines; the softness of the dirt between your fingers. The clean, clear blue sky. Or curled up with hot cocoa by the fire as it crackles and roars and raindrops pelt the window — there was a book on your lap but you watched the flames dance instead. Or in the forest, where it smelled wet and mossy. You watched the bubbles and undulations in the creek, traipsed through the ferns, admired the eagles soaring above your head. Just being a kid was probably the most romantic time in most of our lives. Unhurried, dawdling, captivated by the moment: romance is like seeing the world through the eyes of a child.

Senya was nonetheless vague with her sage words. She did not lay it all out like that. She left us to figure that part out on our own. It was a learning process but our lives are fuller now because of it. I may not have a lover but my life does not lack romance. I make time to be with me and drink it all in. The ruins of abandoned buildings. The creek side paths and bridges to nowhere. The electricity of the city. The fireflies that zip and hover over the boardwalk. It is safe to say, the most romantic moments of my life were not conceived with a partner. Moments I would have missed out on if I waited for someone else to join me.

It is our duty to pass Senya's wisdom on like the gift that it is, share it with anyone who is waiting for romance to come to them. Romance is not as narrow as dinner and a movie, diamond rings, or vacations in Hawaii. It is not an activity just for two. It does not have to lead to wedding bells or any kind of commitment except an agreement to be open to it wherever it finds you.

Romance can be a lot of things. It can be a horse-drawn carriage ride with your lover. But it doesn't have to be. It can be a picnic in a meadow, but it does not have to be that either. It can be a dozen red roses but it can also be the moss on the side of an old stone building. It can be a heart shaped chocolate sampler but I think it is more likely to be the rainbow that shines through the canyon at Silver Falls. Romance comes in many forms. That's what Senya says.

This is an expanded version of Senya Says. A shorter version originally appeared in the January 7, 2014 issue of The Paperbook Collective.

Quick Flicks—dark comedy in a flash

Zoey & Katy

The uniform is the worst part of the job: starched button up, stiff, itchy collar. It's wet in no time, heavy with the salty drops that fall off the back of my head. The bowtie around my neck is too tight and soon it is also soaking wet. The black polyester slacks trap heat and sweat in the space between my balls and ass crack. It is a ridiculous masochistic thing to wear under the angry yellow flame of the Los Angeles sun but I suffer for the honor of serving celebrities and socialites cocktails on platinum trays.

At least they don't make us wear jackets. My friend Rico works for a company that makes them wear jackets. The thermometer by the bar says 93. I would die if I had to wear a jacket.

Even if you forget the uniform this job is not as glamorous as they claimed. *Hob knob with the stars! Serve premium food and drinks to celebrities at high end events.* Except what the ad really meant is that we may as well be robots or strategically placed drink stands for all the actual hob knobbing we do.

If I sweat much more the martinis on my tray are going to be dirty instead of dry.

But if I wear anything less formal, anything remotely comfortable then, well then they will notice me. Or if I gain a few pounds, maybe a gut, a couple inches around the waist, they will definitely notice me then and they will complain to the maître d' about my offensiveness and I will be on the unemployment line before the night is over.

Of course they don't hold themselves to the same standards. And it is not just the meat dresses and accidental exposures that I'm talking about. What you see on TV, in the movies, online, that is not what they really look like. The real pictures, the true to life versions, only show up in tabloid magazines.

Before I started this job there was a rumor around town that Katy Perry and Zoey Deschanel are the same person. My spank bank threatened to shrink by one. If I only knew. . .

The first event I ever worked was a shock. *Where are all of the beautiful people?* I searched for them, but they were nowhere to be found. The whole point of taking this job was so that I could check out J Lo, Halle Berry, Angelina Jolie, you get the picture, right? But there wasn't no J Lo up in that place, no sir! J Lo's heinous inbred cousin maybe, but not the real J Lo! See, there is a difference between a nice, big juicy booty and something that could take out a city block if it backs up too fast. Halle Berry wasn't there either, unless you were looking for the unblinking, bucktooth version. And Angelina Jolie? Talk about an old lady with tattoo regret.

It wasn't them. It couldn't be them. I had to be at the wrong party.

"Hey Juan," I said to the bartender as I waited for him to refill my tray. "What's up? I thought we were working a Hollywood party?"

"We are dude," he chuckled. "This is it." He pointed at the buffet. There was a sloppy man with a whole cheese tray resting on his gut. "That's Mel Gibson."

After a few months I guess I got used to looking at them, knowing the truth, knowing their photo shopped beauty is worshiped and praised with millions. Not that I don't still hope to see one, just one hot star. Britney Spears maybe? Nope. She's got a neck like a giraffe. Two feet long. Not kidding. Pamela Anderson? Now that is one hot plastic jigsaw mess. One by one each celebrity bubble has burst. The only hot people at these parties are the help and the occasional groupie lucky enough to snag a spot on the arm of some fugly superstar.

Oh and Zoey and Katy? Same damn person. I'm looking right at her, just served her a drink. And she doesn't belong in anybody's spank bank.

Bones and Silicone

Grave robbing in southern California was all Leroy's idea. "All them rich folk in Cali-Fornia, we could make a fortune!" He tilted the bottle back and stared up at the stars, "You know them rich people, they so greedy, they so scared somebody else gonna get they stuff they even take it to the grave with 'em."

Wide eyed with a shit eating grin, I lapped up his every word. "Like them pharaohs back in Egypt?" I asked.

"Just like them pharaohs." Leroy was the smartest guy I ever met. His parents were only second cousins.

"You reckon we'll find mummies in there with 'em too?"

He laughed and I felt my face get hot and sheepish. "Ain't no such thing as mummies," he said. "That there is an urban myth. Everybody know that." He tilted the bottle back again and then offered it to me. "You old enough now boy."

My hands shook as I reached out for it, as I put it to my lips. My tongue trembled under the first sip then went numb under the second and third.

"You like that?" he beamed big and toothless. "That there's some primo shine right there. G'head, have some more."

So I did. And that was how I came to follow Leroy down the mountain and out west to Hollywood. We hitchhike the whole way there; from Arkansas to Los Angeles, mostly truckers with heavy breath and wandering hands. Leroy always makes me sit in the middle. When we get to the big city it is already dusk.

Perfect time to get straight to work.

Graveyards out here are lot fancier than back home. "All's my pappy got was a cross made outta two sticks," I moan, kicking a marble headstone.

Leroy pierces the manicured earth with his shovel. "You's could always take your pappy this here one. If'ns you can carry it I mean."

It takes a lot of digging to get into the grave. We haven't even reached the casket yet and I'm in over my head. "Leroy you sure we's doin' this right? We ain't never had to dig this far before."

He chuckles and says, "They got earth quakes round here boy. Gotta put 'em real deep or every time it shakes there'd be bodies poppin' up outta the ground. Wouldn't wanna see that now would ya?"

"No sir," I shake my head. "No I wouldn't." A half hour later my shovel finally makes a THUD! I look up at Leroy pride on my face, "That it? That it? Did I hit it? That's it huh?"

He smiles wide and jumps knees clear to his elbows. When he lands the space under his feet sounds almost hollow. "That's it!" A few more shovelfuls and he is on his hands and knees prying the lid off of the casket. I press my face in close and he tells me to stand back. "Out the way boy!" The wood creaks and sighs and fights against him until he stands back up, one hand on his hip, the other wiping sweat from his brow. "Damn it! I never seen a grave so hard to rob before."

"You want me to get the crow bar?" I offer.

"Yeah," he nods. "Yeah that's a good idea." But even with the crow bar the lid doesn't come right up. Instead pieces chip off bit by bit. Still, he is relentless, determined to cash in. He hacks away at the casket, faster and faster, until finally a hole pokes through. "Hey boy," he yells. "Bring that gosh darn flashlight. Hurry up!" Excitement rushes through me as I picture jewels and gold and cash money that are about to be ours. I rush over to the hard won peep hole and shine the light towards it. But before I can see in Elroy wrestles it out of my hands. "Gimme that." He lowers himself onto his hands and knees, aims the light onto our treasures below. Silence. He doesn't say anything. No whooping. No hollering.

"What's in there?" I beg. "What do you see?"

No celebrating. He stands up, leaving the flashlight on the roof of the casket, and hoists himself out of the grave without a word. A few steps and it is in my hand. I kneel over the ragged hole. But there are no rubies or diamonds or pearls, no gold bars or hundred dollar bills, all there are, is bones and silicone.

God on You Tube

The instant messenger chimed just as God was about to solve three down in the Sunday crosswords. It was a hard one too. Thirteen letters. Rain is a type of this.

Ding ding.

Fifth letter was 'i'. It was just on the tip of His tongue.

Ding ding.

God turned to face the monitor. As the avatar in the messenger box came into focus through His cataracts He sighed and rolled His eyes. Satan. Always goofing around. He was almost afraid to read what His best friend/nemesis had written. Half the time when He clicked on the window a pair of fake boobs would pop onto His screen. The other half, Satan just needed to borrow a few bucks to keep the lights on down below.

"You've got to see this!" Then there was a link. Followed by, "Seriously, check it out."

Yup, tits, thought God. He clicked on the link anyway but, instead of the surgically implanted silicone and rock hard nipples that Satan preferred to His real creations, the screen was filled with a rainbow colored fro. *What in the hell?*

As if he had read the supreme being's mind, Satan typed back, "Not hell. Pittsburg."

God leaned forward in His office chair and rested His elbows on the desk. He watched as the video panned back to reveal a man with his face painted blue and a belly distended by too much beer and red meat. It pulled back still more to show a crudely painted sign, also in rainbow letters. A simple sign, it read: John 3:16. That's it. Nothing more. The Father in Heaven buried His head in His hands.

Below, Satan grabbed his belly, aching with laughter. "Oh man." He cackled as he typed. "They sure know how to make you look stupid!"

It was true. His followers had done some pretty embarrassing things in His name. Except, as He explained to His favorite frenemy, "That's not even the worst of it."

Precipitation. God spun around in His chair, back to the crossword puzzle, and wrote the word in the proper spaces. The messenger chimed again.

"Hey you had a good run," the Devil empathized. "Anyways it's probably just a fad."

"Easy for you to say," God typed back. While His followers were busy making asses of themselves, Satanists everywhere were fighting for inclusive religious policies and embarrassing Christians who refused to recognize that school prayers to Jesus and stone altars featuring the ten commandments on government property as the violations of the separation of church and state that they are. And of course it wasn't just the Christians. Fundamentalist Islam had become quite the thorn in His side. For once He was glad that the world's monotheistic religions still had not realized they were all worshipping the same god. Then there were the Mormons, who were blaming Him for the weird magical underwear they force each other to wear. God, the Mormons. All He needed now was for the Jehovah Witnesses to start acting up.

God sighed and clicked on another video. The screen filled with angry people thumping protest signs as He typed back, "I should have listened to my parents and been a bodhisattva instead."

With another *ding* the messenger pops up: "LMFAO! Right. Like you could handle NOT being the center of the universe . . ."

God stared at the dismembered fetus on His screen and grimaced. He knew for a fact that it was computer generated, not the product of an abortion, but it didn't matter. Sick to His stomach He clicked on another video, this one with His name in the title. Before it began He started typing, "Can't you get your guys to act out again for a while? Maybe burn some virgins or something and give me a break?" He shouldn't have to beg. The Devil definitely owed Him one. Or three. Or a hundred. Another iPhone movie took over His screen. God watched as at least ten men beat one of His children to a bloody pulp. The video ended with the caption in red, "God hates fags." Without waiting for a response, He sent another message, "The things they do in my name makes me sick."

"Maybe it's time to rein them in."

God read the IM fast, too fast, and did a double take. He typed quickly and had to go back and correct more than one typo. "You mean like in Revelations? You can't be serious!" But the more He thought about it the more convinced He became. It was time. Time to rain down fire and brimstone on all the humans who maimed and murdered and otherwise made assholes out of themselves for His benefit.

"What? No! Chill out dude. I just meant like a few really bad storms or tsunamis or something. Geez you and the . . ."

But when God shut off His monitor and went back to His crossword puzzle He knew. Five across. Eleven words. Last letter 'n', first letter 't'.

Tribulation.

Sucky Sucky, Part One

Since the dawn of the human race we have stared out at the skies, at the stars in the black expanse of space, and wondered — is there anybody else out there?

We always assumed that if there were they would be smarter than us, more advanced, so advanced, in fact, that they no longer needed opposable thumbs or body hair. They would arrive in shiny space disks that travel faster than the speed of light, their technology millennia more advanced than our own. Maybe they would be friendly and come to save us from some sort of earth destroying catastrophe. Maybe they would come to kill us all and take over our planet. Or, maybe they just stick with kidnapping a few rednecks here and there and sticking probes up their butts for shits and giggles.

But we never ever (ever!) thought we would be the ones to find them. Humans were never really known for our smarts after all, even among ourselves. I mean shit, Tinurtia had been hiding behind Mars the whole time!

Tinurtia — a moon with an atmosphere much like the Earths. It would be cold, but the air was safe to breathe. NASA didn't waste any time on unmanned flights. They sent us in, boots on the ground, first thing. I volunteered. History in the making baby!

After landing, everyone gathered at the back door and waited for it to be lowered. All elbows and heels, we crowded round as the heavy metal door started to creak and moan. We all wanted to be the first to set eyes on this alien moon that had embarrassed so many great astronomers with its discovery, but none of us were prepared for what we were about to see.

Little green women.

All around me there were gasps. Jaws dropped. Soldiers and scientists alike muttered what the fucks. I couldn't help it, I smiled. What? She had big tits! Ok, they were green but tits are tits!

I pushed past my captain, that goofy grin still plastered on my face, and started down the ramp. He probably wanted to call out to me, scream at me to wait for orders, but his big square jaw was frozen open so I kept going until I stepped out onto Tinurtia's soil. There had to be twenty women in front of me, not one over four feet tall. They were green from head to toe and they were bald just like in all the alien stories, but that's where the similarities ended. Their big black eyes were framed by big black lashes and their shiny heads were no more out of proportion to their bodies than the average little person back home. Instead of hair they had antennas, two or three inches long, on either side of their head, and on the end of each antenna was something round and concave like a suction cup. On closer look they had those same suction cups on the tips of their fingers and the bottoms of their toes. The one in front, the one with the huge green tits spilling out of her torn crop top, opened her mouth to speak and there was even one on the end of her tongue. Blood rushed to the tip of my nub and it was easy as pie to ignore her rotten jags of brown and gold chompers.

The little green women invited us back home with them, to a hamlet in the dusty hills. They cooked us a dinner heavy in greasy meat and tubers they fried over a campfire. We never found out what kind of meat it was or saw any of their men, and nobody ever talked about either. It was hard to care. I mean, here they were serving us this feast, who were we to ask questions? And every time one of them bent over the table with a fresh plate her big bouncy tits were just centimeters from our faces, no more than a stained wife beater between us.

The soldier beside me elbowed me in the ribs. When I looked over at him his eyes were wild, his face contorted in excitement. "Imagine what a blow job from one of those bitches would be like!" He threw his head back and laughed like an animal.

I wanted to know too. Shit, I'm a man ain't I? And I was going to find out.

But not before the little green women cleared the dishes and returned with jugs of clear liquid that smelled like jet fuel. The front woman from when we landed, she climbed right up on my lap, her bony ass digging into me in a painfully delicious way that left my stiffy lodged in the space between her legs. Not inside of her — yet — just nestled near and ready. My uniform was still in the way of course, but I'm pretty sure she was bare under her mini skirt. She put the jug up to my lips and tilted it back. Whatever it was, it burned my throat and set my belly on fire. I coughed and sputtered.

All around, my fellow soldiers whooped and hollered as the little green women climbed onto their laps. Most of them took the moonshine better than I did, probably because they knew what to expect after watching me. The guy next to me called, "Hey look at this!" I did and saw that he had pulled one of the alien's tits out of her shirt. Instead of a nipple, she had a suction cup. He poked at it and it fluttered. He stuck his finger in the middle of the cup and it wrapped itself around the tip of his finger. I could hear the sucking, like a baby with a bottle, from where I sat. The soldier bounced in his chair and the alien bounced on his lap. "Can you imagine?" Then he leaned forward over her legs and started to whisper, as if it was our little secret. "Can you imagine if they have the same thing down there?" He sniggered as he said it, pointed to the spot between her legs.

Hells yeah I could imagine. I ignored him and turned back to the babe on my own lap. I asked her if she wanted to go for a walk and even though she couldn't understand me, she looked at me dreamily so I put one arm under her knees and the other around her shoulders and stood up. Hoots and hollers followed us into the bushes.

And yes. She did have a suction cup for a vagina.

Holeeeeeeeee fuck.

Sex Drugs & Alco-mo-hol—shorts on the line

Necromancing—surviving singledom in the 21ˢᵗ century

It is like waking up from the dead. Like you were so deep, so deep in there that you forgot you were alive. It is like you were so fucked up you forgot you existed and you should be glad that you are still breathing but really you are just surprised. You REALLY expected to be dead. You really felt like it was all over. And THAT, that is what makes you feel alive to begin with.

The moment your eyes pop open everything is bright, way too bright. Your contacts are dry, they feel rigid; shrink wrapped around your corneas. You want to take them out but are afraid they will take your pupils with them. You are not in your own bed.

Sigh.

It is always better that way. Except… You don't know where the fuck you are.

You roll over to find a ginger with the body of a demigod. You wish you could remember what he was like but you fucked up again, got too drunk. You weren't even in and out this time. It is like you were never there. It happens more and more but it is such a fine line between getting drunk enough to get laid but not so drunk to black out… at least completely.

You sit up, silent. Try not to wake whoever that is. You scan the room for your clothes and find everything except your underwear. Shit. You get up, start to dress. Could he have snatched them up earlier? Like a trophy… Where would he have stashed them?

Or maybe you didn't wear any last night. Shit. You stare at the ceiling, thinking. The last thing you remember is... the kitchen? Taking hits of homegrown off of a cheap mass manufactured glass pipe and drinking Budweiser from a can. No. No, there is more. Stumbling down the stairs. Then one of those drunken pisses that never seems to end. And that's it. The freckled lips grumble from the bed, his nostrils flare hard like a horse, his naked body trembles in the cold. You pray he is not waking up.

Fuck it. You dress, leave whatever panties you may have been wearing behind and grab your phone, your purse, your keys. You search the room for the exit but there are only stairs going up. Somehow you have found yourself in an aboveground sunlit basement. It isn't possible but you clamber up the stairs anyway, down a dim hallway and out into the early morning sun.

Outside, your disorientation worsens. Where the fuck are you? It is bright and you squint as you put the key in the ignition and pull out onto the road with a filthy windshield and the realization that you are still very much fuckered up.

Just make it home. Go slow. Keep it straight. Don't get pulled over. You promise you will never do it again. You will be more responsible.

The truth is you need it. Ok not quite like this, you would rather remember it. But you do crave it. And you are not alone in desperate stilettos and a give it to me mini dress. There is a whole flock of girls vying for attention. Boosted on neo martinis, Xanax, Ritalin, cocaine, Redbull, all of you strain to be just interesting enough, just exciting enough that someone okay looking will take you home. Of course the whole thing about the bar scene is not that beer goggles make the losers look any better. The whole thing about the bar scene is that around 1:45 am you go to the washroom and look into the mirror under the harsh fluorescent light and instead of the fox that sauntered into the club earlier that night, what you see through those beer goggles is a haggard desperate broad that would be lucky to leave with the homeless guy hanging around outside.

At that point almost anyone will do. And the sad reality, that it is all really up to them, and they would never choose you sober, it makes you angry but only for a moment. Survival is more important. It is basic biology.

Biology. Sometimes the hole just needs to get filled. Beer Goggles don't take away the layer of hair on his back or the belly that hides his penis or that needy face you would rather forget. But you do not see any of that because you're too busy counting your lucky starts that this guy will let you scream and moan and bounce around on something for a while goddamnit. You are just getting into it when conk you are asleep and then conk again your dear friend is outside that stranger's bedroom door knocking and whispering and calling that it is time to leave she has kids to pick up and all of that jazz..

You would be a terrible friend except that you are just a product of society and everyone knows that all friends everywhere have a duty, not just to never interfere in their friends getting laid, but to facilitate it in any way possible. Even at the expense of their own families. Cockblocking is not just a strict no-no, it almost goes against the rules of the new sisterhood.

Only half way out, a stranger's bed is such sweet suicide. It is a chance you take. A chance that makes you feel alive. He COULD wrap his hands around your neck and squeeze. He could bash your head against the concrete ground. He could force you to react to him. He could force you to kill him in the most brutal of ways. He could force you to rake your teeth across his skull while you press the magic button that stops his heart.

It is all chance. Like the lottery.

Any one of them could have left you in a ditch to die. Good thing they were decent-ish guys. Decent-ish… It is a fine line between date rape and a ploy to get fucked after all. How are they supposed to know the difference?

Do they even care?

Do you?

Drugs are what you have to do to get him… and him, and him, every notch on your bedpost the result of some sort of cocktail. Vodka Redbull cocaine marijuana Cosmopolitan Percocet Ritalin dust. Cocktails lead to cock tales. It is the reason you party all the time.

Of course you talk about it. You compete. You stack numbers. You give them degrading nicknames and plot on how to take advantage of them. You trade places in dark rooms. It is only fair.

COCK TALES.

Why play a dating game where commitment beyond tomorrow night is unfathomable? Why waste your time looking for Mr. Right when what you need is Mr. Right Now? Why search out some knight in shining armor when all that is left are necromancers?

It's the second half of that word that bothers you, not the dead part, the romancing part. The part that wants to whisper in your ear and the kiss your neck. You wish they would cut out all the bullshit but you put up with it to get to the good stuff. The pump pump bang bang slappity slap.

The reason they like you is you're never too with it, you're never too there. Isn't it ironic? They think they get you drunk to take advantage of YOU. They love to hear you say let's get fucked up tonight and know they don't even have to buy your drinks. Forty dollars lighter, you are way more fun. Blacked out you are the life of the party. So you die and die and die again. Your body has more rhythm, your brain has more wit, your lips spit more funny on autopilot anyway.

Necromancing: surviving singledom in the 21st century originally appeared in the Fall 2013 issue of Dirty Chai Magazine.

The Necromancer Within

You know the other side of the story. Most gen x and millennial women probably do. Getting drunk, snorting coke, popping pills. Dressing like a skank. Making out with other girls on the dance floor. It is a lot of work trying to get laid.

Ain't that the sad truth.

It starts hours before the night is even born. Tweeze, shave, and wax away everything below your scalp. Exfoliate, tan, moisturize. Wash, dry, and fry your hair straight, curl your eyelashes and cover your face in war paint. Sometimes it is a group effort, a herd of girls plucking and primping and sucking in their guts between pre-game shots.

Shots! Shots! Shots!

You dress each other in skimpiness bought with maxed out plastic. You spend this month's electric bill on heels and party favors. Who cares about tomorrow? You are alive right now!

YOLO!

So take another shot, have another martini, maybe a Percocet or some E, do a line in the ladies' room. Flirt and dance, fall down, get back up and black out, wake up in a stranger's bed. Live to do it all over again.

No one ever said all that hard work wasn't fun. Young and dumb and full of cum, it's a blast in more ways than one. What is that they say about working hard and playing harder? That is singledom sex in a nutshell.

Critics will call you a slut. Say you're pathetic for using chemicals to enhance your personality. But you know all about them and you don't give a fuck. Like I said, you already know that side of the story.

What I really want to know is, do you know about this side too?

What side?

This side. Their side.

Their side?

You know. The necromancers' side. I can see it on your face, in your eyes. You've seen it from their side. You've cast their spells, you've ravaged the dead.

What? Me? No. Never!

Oh so I suppose you just happened to be standing there when he fell off the bar stool and into your arms? And you just happened to be there when he needed help to the urinal? The better question is, of course, why didn't you just hold it for him?

Maybe he wasn't ready. Maybe he needed another beer. And you were quick to get it for him, along with a shot of Jack to chase it all down. Don't worry. Shoot, I am not judging. If anything I have a high five for you, a pat on the back. Still, why deny premeditation? There is no good reason to disavow the game. All's fair in drugs and necrophilia as long as it's consensual.

But that is where the line gets blurry, isn't it? How do you tell between the guy that guzzles to calm his performance anxiety and the one that would have said no if he could have?

That's rich. Now that the shoe is on the other foot…

Ok, true, you got me there. So you pick your poison and ply your mark. It is not like he resists much anyway. He is little and pretty, almost too pretty. The little part is vital; he cannot weigh much more than you, just in case you have to drag him back to your cave at the end of the night. And he is so pretty word around town is he bats for the other team, but you figure that just makes it a challenge. Even better, he can't hold his liquor. But you can. So you slurp 'em up, dare him to match you drink for drink.

Geez, not like I roofied him.

Sure hope not. Dead in the head drunk is one thing, fucking a corpse is whole other.

He was a VERY willing participant…

That he was. He may not have made the first move, but after you jumped on him it was on. He stuck his tongue in your mouth and his hands under your shirt. He stripped and tossed you down on the mattress. He climbed on your chest and shoved his dick down your throat.

See! I told you.

You told me and a lot of other people too. Just like you always run and tell about all of your latest conquests, the newest rungs carved above your bed. You always have a competition running. Neck and neck with your bestest girlfriend for this month's prize. Not many girls think to take on the necromancer's role; they are already so used to playing dead. This strategy, well it just might put you in the lead, it just might put you aHEAD.

And it might be better to keep your tactic a secret but you brag willy nilly instead. End of the workday, you join the boys trading battle stories. But your story? Your story is met with stony silence. They do not appreciate the tables being turned. They don't see it your way. "So you raped him?" the fat kid says.

Not anymore than you raped me.

It is one of your dirtiest secrets, so you only think it. Yeah you messed around with him one desperate night. You do not want anyone to know. I am sure you are thankful to be reminded that he was your necromancer for a few drunken moments before you realized his tits were bigger than yours.

Double standard.

It is.

Not like I am one of those musty beasts that plants herself on random dicks while they are passed out.

I hear you. But still…

Still what?

That pretty boy never called you.

So?

Didn't he ignore your texts? Didn't he even… hide from you? After? Like a mouse keeps away from a cat…

Sounds like typical post-coital male behavior…

Ah touché, you have me again! But to duck into an alcove and literally quiver in his One Stars until you pass? Don't you think…well… maybe it's better to preserve some innocence? Once you adopt their ways, once you cross over, once you become one of them… a full-fledged necromancer… what is left of your human side?

Eat It

He checks his phone compulsively as seconds, then minutes, drag on. His foot taps, anxious that she has not responded. The meeting draws to a close and Daniel finds himself back at his desk, pretending to process medical benefits while he waits. And waits. Her one-word answer arrives as the work day draws to an end: "Maybe."

Maybe. When it comes to coke maybe means hope. If it were anything else, of course, he would automatically assume the worst.

The rest of the evening passes in nervous anticipation, and he is unable to concentrate on anything else. One too many texts to check her progress and Tina sends back a scathing diatribe about how she has to talk to someone at the bar about it and it probably won't be a problem but if he really wants it he better chill out and wait patiently or he can just forget about it. Daniel hisses to himself and mumbles something about PMS as he reads.

With this and each passing moment, his hope sours. It isn't until after he has given up entirely, shut off the TV and proceeded with his nightly rituals, that the response finally comes. He is in the middle of flossing, the waxy string stuck between two molars, when there is a knock on his door. He is annoyed and relieved at the same time. And also thankful that she doesn't arrive twenty minutes later when his hands will be in his pants instead of his mouth.

"Geez, about time," he complains with gratitude.

"Yeah, yeah." She rolls her bloodshot eyes and saunters in. Kicking her shoes off at the door, she reminds him that unless he can get his own he might want to tone down his attitude. She speaks with effort, with obvious concentration.

"You're drunk!" Daniel accuses.

"What?" she scoffs, plopping down on the couch.

"Am not!"

"You're slurring!"

"I am not!"

"I like drunk Tina," he grins.

"I am not drunk!"

"Oh, OK." Then, he whispers, "Drunk Tina . . ."

"I had a couple of drinks while I was waiting, but I am not drunk!"

The evening has turned out to have a lot more potential than he could have anticipated but he has to play it just right. Tina can be pliable. When she wants to be. It is rare, but when it happens Daniel knows he has a chance. And the more chances he adds up, few and far between as they are, the better a shot he has in the long run. If only he can get her to mess around with him enough times, whatever that tipping point is, when they reach it she will give up the fight and settle down with him. It makes sense, sort of.

"So . . ." he says.

"Soooooo?"

"Soooooo . . . how about that package?"

"Soooooo . . . how about that money?"

"Shoot!" But he stops short at Tina's raised eyebrows. Hands on his hips, he just stares at the floor.

"Did you forget the money or something?"

"No," he chides, "I was just hoping you would cover it this time."

"You're weird," she hisses, a half-laugh, half-sneer on her face.

"What? It's your turn."

She huffs, "My turn?"

"Yeah, I always buy it."

"It's for you!"

"Yeah, but you do it too."

"Only cause it's there, it's free; I would never pay for it!"

"But it's not free. You should have to pay for it too."

"I'm getting it for you! I'm risking a felony for something I wouldn't otherwise be doing! Sharing is the least you can do. Shit, I should charge you a finder's fee!"

He has played it wrong. He was trying to be funny, tease her a little, but instead she is mad. Daniel grabs his wallet from the kitchen counter and takes out a stack of twenties. "Sorry. There's a hundred and forty," he says, his head hanging low as he hands over the wad.

"Fine," she mumbles. She does not offer the extra twenty dollars back, but his passive aggressive behavior still manages to make her feel a little guilty about keeping it.

He offers her a drink and she accepts a Captain and Coke before he sits down to chop up a few lines. Daniel is methodical, almost obsessive, about his cocaine and, as much as she despises rum, she knows she will need something to keep her buzz going while she waits. She has brought along certain intentions, realized halfway through her fourth gin and tonic at the bar, and she does not want to sober up enough to recognize how errant they are. So she stirs and does more than sip, determined to keep up her resolve. It has been months since she has been laid. It is simply biological: she needs dick and Daniel will just have to do. It isn't like they have never done it before. And she will get good and drunk so that it won't be too weird.

She is nearly done with her drink by the time Daniel brushes the powder into four lines. While he does it, he explains what brought on his sudden insistence for narcotics. "That's ridiculous," Tina says, rolling her eyes. "Drugs make the world go 'round. What are they going to do, piss test the whole world?"

"Sally would if she could! And we're talking about state employees here. People hate us! We're right there next to pedophiles and welfare queens. If she got it on the ballot, voters would go for it!"

"You really think she would take it that far? Do you have any idea how much work that is?" Tina is in one of her bossier know-it-all drunk moods.

He wishes she were in one of her sultry, sensual drunk moods instead. But it is now or never so he pushes forward anyway. "You know, it would be great if I could do a line off your tits this time."

Blank poker face, she considers the option. Does she really want to do this? Daniel interprets her silence as rejection and apologizes. To his surprise, she yanks her T-shirt over her head and pulls her breasts out of her bra. "Go ahead." He freezes, convinced that he must be in the middle of a dream that will shatter to pieces the moment he makes a move towards her. "What are you waiting for?"

Daniel shakes his head. Now or never, he tells himself. He moves towards her, a CD case covered with blow in one hand. He still feels it is the best surface for chopping, even if it is outdated technology. He holds the case up against her left breast and uses his credit card to brush the first line onto her soft, supple flesh, sure that none of this is really happening. Still, he struggles with the impending bulge in his pants. Control yourself, he demands, scrunching his eyes shut for a second.

"You OK?" It is a question formed in impatience, not concern.

"Yeah, yeah, I'm great. Just a lot of anticipation," he says. "Wow." Finally, he grabs a short length of drinking straw that he keeps just for such occasions. He leans over and puts the straw between his right nostril and the messy pile of powder on her breast. He places a finger over his other nostril and inhales. If Sally has her way at least his last time will be the best time.

He leaves a dusting of residue just above her nipple. She knows what comes next and she will savor it. She needs it. Daniel leans forward and opens his mouth. Slowly, so nervous his tongue shakes, he licks the powder from her creamy flesh. She closes her eyes and focuses on the sensation. He continues to lick, downward, toward her nipple. Out of nowhere he drops a rock onto it, which he suckles off. She responds with heavy breathing and a near moan, sure signs that she is game after all, so he cups her other breast in his hand and kneads it softly.

Tina moans again but then suddenly bolts up. "Where's my line?"

"Right here." He offers her the CD case and the half-straw.

She snorts like a pro, boobs still hanging out over her bra, and traipses into the kitchen where she takes the Jäger from the freezer and a shot glass from the cupboard. She pours herself a shot, slams it, and stalks only semi-sexily back to the living room without offering Daniel any.

"You're welcome," he says with a half-laugh.

"Yeah, thanks," she says, pushing him back in his chair. She straddles him so that her breasts are once again level with his mouth and when he opens his mouth to speak she shoves her other tit in. "Harder," she commands. So he sucks and nibbles as he strokes her breasts, her ass, her thighs, rubbing and squeezing. She leans backwards, spine arched, and starts to gyrate on his lap. "Harder!" she says again.

He tries to hide his growing discomfort. He can't miss this opportunity. Still, Tina is not just demanding, she is downright mean. She knows what she wants and she wants it right away. When she decides it is time for oral she climbs off of him, turns around, and rips her pants off. She grabs her ankles and pushes her ass in his face. "Lick my pussy!"

He does as he is told. The tip of his nose rubs between her cheeks. He can only hope she showered since her last shit. Daniel isn't turned on anymore; he just wants to make it out in one piece. When it is time to put it in, he claims to be unprepared.

"What the fuck? How do you not have a condom?"

"Why would I? I never get laid!"

"Because you don't have condoms!" she retorts.

"You don't either!"

"I don't have a penis!" Tina stands in front of him, hands on her hips, mad as hell. She taps her foot. "I need to get off."

"I can pull out . . ."

"No," she interrupts. "God knows what you could have picked up from Cindi."

"That's not very nice." His voice is low, not more than a tremble, meek in her shadow.

"Just being real," she snaps. "You're going to have to eat it real good." She climbs back onto the couch, her feet on either side of him, her pussy in his face. "Lean back," she instructs. But his soft approach only aggravates her more. Taking matters into her own hands, she lifts her left leg up onto the back of the couch and grinds against his face.

Daniel struggles to breathe as juices and mucus membranes envelope his mouth and nose. He prays that she will get off quickly. Only once before has he been in such a hurry for it to be over, and that was when Cindi came after him with a coy smile and a strap-on.

Untitled is an excerpt from the novel Suicide in Tiny Increments by Riya Anne Polcastro.

Dive Bar Blues Tales

FlashFiction by Riya Anne Polcastro

Why I Need a Sex Robot

I'm wiping down the bar just before close, ready for this twelve hour shift to end already. There are still a few stragglers left: a couple of lottery players, a smoker on the back porch, and a shaggy guy my age at the bar watching me in that way that makes me roll my eyes and gag a little. I traipse back to the kitchen and take my time washing the night's dishes. Hopefully he finishes his beer and leaves before I am done back here.

No such luck. When I go back out front one of the lottery players is gone, and from the video feed it looks like the smoker is too, but Shaggy's still here, past last call, his beer glass clearly empty. I start flicking off the neons. Most people get the hint at that point. The last lottery player leaves.

"Alright buddy, time to go," I say when it's obvious he hasn't figured it out.

"Yeah I know," he sighs. "I just wanted to ask you something."

Ugh. I know what's coming. Every female bartender knows what's coming. Probably every female everywhere knows what's coming . . .

"Can I take you out sometime?"

I just stare at him. Blank. Poker face.

"A couple drinks or something?"

"I gotta lock up so if you could leave now that would be great."

"So is that a no?"

"Uh, yeah that's definitely a no."

"C'mon, what do you have to lose?"

If I wasn't somewhat homicidal myself I might think my life, I could lose my life. I pay attention to the headlines. I read Jezebel. I know the risk women take when they go out with strange men. Any men really. Plenty of predators are already familiar with their victims.

But no, that wouldn't be a fair answer because, let's be quite honest, I wouldn't hesitate to shank this guy with his own screwdriver if I needed to. Besides, it isn't fear at all that motivates me to reject Shaggy. Instead it's a been there done that, learned my lesson too many times kind of thing. You see, no matter how cute this boy may be with his hair hanging in his bright blue eyes, no matter how good he may or may not be in bed, no matter how convincing he is that that isn't or is all he wants depending on what I want, it's still the same old, same old. Tired. Game.

And more than anything guess what? I don't owe this guy an explanation! He is not entitled to a date with me UNLESS I can come up with an explanation that meets whatever his litmus test is for a reasonable reason to reject him.

"Bye," I wave, not bothering to fake a smile.

"Really?" he whines. "You really won't even give me a shot?'

Since when did this shit become a negotiation? Since when did "No" come to mean badger me until I say yes to shut you up? "Good. Bye."

I'm pretty sure I hear him mutter "Bitch" under his

breath as he stomps away. Then, after he opens the door to leave, he turns back to me and says, loud and clear, "You're a fucking man hater."

Oh wow. Oh wow oh wow oh wow. I laugh. I laugh so hard I almost cry. He said man-hater like it's MY fault HE is a douchebag.

And that, my friends, is exactly why I don't date men.

Ok, for now. I have. I may in the future. I'd rather not but needs are needs and I'm like a nympho trying to walk in asexual shoes.

You see, it's not the sex I hate. And, despite recent accusations, I don't actually hate men. Like most women, I'm just sick of the bullshit. Sick of the joblessness; sick of the thirty-somethings living at home with Mommy; sick of female best friends not so secretly in love with him (or him with her); sick of guys inviting us out only to think that it means either A. we're going Dutch or B. if they pay we better put out (which even if I wanted to the fuck if I'm going to feel obligated); sick of booty calls who play mind games and make love when they're supposed to fuck; sick of cheaters; sick of guys so addicted to their video games that we are forced to cheat; sick of messy motherfuckers who expect us to clean up after them; sick of bringing home half the income and doing all the housework; sick, sick, sick . . .

And that, my friends, is why I need a Sex Robot.

A whaaaat? A sex robot!

Ok, ok, it's not a real thing. Yet! But come on, if there was ever a good use for artificial intelligence this is it! And come on ladies, admit it, we'd get a lot more done if we weren't so frustrated, if we didn't waste so much time on men who either can't perform or break our hearts without a second thought. We could even, dare I say, finally take over the world?

Imagine it. All the sex you want without any of that bullshit. No losers to wade through. No bitches to compete with. No egos to stroke. No dirty boxers to pick up off the floor.

No diseases to worry about.

And you could custom order him. No more trying to determine if those are pecs or man boobs under baggy t-shirts. No more trying to guess the size of his penis by how big his hands and feet are.

No more settling.

Exactly what you want. In a box. There when you need him, put away in the closet when you don't. He'll never embarrass you in public with his flatulent outbursts or try to sleep with your friends. If you want to make love, he'll make love to you. If you want to fuck, he'll fuck.

He'll learn what you like. He'll learn where to pump, where to rub, where to swivel. He'll learn how. What. When. When you want multiples and when you want simultaneous orgasms.

And if even robot sex is too monogamous? Change his face. Change his body. Change his dick. Interchangeable parts would still be cheaper than date night outfits, blowouts, and manicures after all. Mix it up every night of the week. Every hour of the day if you need.

Give us sex robots. Because relationships are overrated. And booty calls are complicated.

Sex robots. So we can get off and focus on the things that matter.

The full collection of Dive Bar Blues Tales can be found at www.divebarbluestales.wordpress.com.

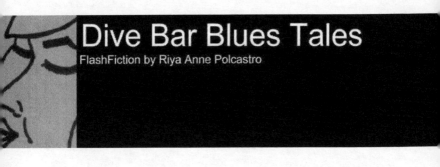

Dive Bar Blues Tales

FlashFiction by Riya Anne Polcastro

Spiked, Part One

Working in this sort of place, getting hit on is just part of the territory. You expect it from everyone because, eventually, even the most platonic customers will get shitfaced enough to confess their undying love for you. It doesn't help being the only woman in the bar, but it isn't just the men and they certainly are not the most aggressive!

Meet Celia, a quiet girl, she comes in with a few friends here and there, drinks a glass of cranberry juice and minds her own business. Then last Saturday, out of nowhere, she decided to match shots with her girls. Bad idea, she could not hang! Three Pink Pussies later and she was perched at the bar, tweeting my ears off until I went for a smoke break. But I still couldn't get away, she followed me outside and that's when she attacked me, pulled me onto her lap and tried to stick her tongue in my ear.

It was funny enough at the time, but now that she is back at the rail again, two Washington Apples down the hatch, I am a little worried that she might make a thing of it. For now she is droning on, god knows about what: her purse dog, shoe collection, favorite musicians, favorite Kardashian, blah, blah, blah, I'm not really listening. I just want her to shut up. She orders another drink and saunters off to the wash room. I grab Charlie's economy size Visine from next to the register. I always chalked the bartenders' revenge up to urban myth, but figure it will be worth a try to get this girl to stop talking without sucking on my face first.

A few people come in and sit down at the lottery machines and I forget about the Visine as I make white Russians and cash tickets for the guys at the machines. But when one o'clock rolls around and they leave for home and their impatient wives, she is still here. Talking at me, smiling like she already knows what my pussy tastes like, until all of a sudden her eyes roll back in her head, she slides off of the bar stool and drops to the floor.

In Noir Time—quick crime fiction

Spiked, Part Two

I had been waiting for that licentious smile of hers to twinge and contort into the unmistakable grimace of someone in a serious panic because, well, she is about to crap her pants. This was not supposed to happen!

I rush out from behind the bar and lean down. Celia isn't moving. Her chest is still, no breath goes in or out of her nose or open lips. I lean down and press two fingers into her neck. No pulse. Shit! I jump up and sprint to the front door, lock it before anyone comes in and spies her there on the ground. I lock all of the doors and start to pace back and forth in front of her body.

What the fuck do I do? Can't call an ambulance, they find Visine in her system guess who the first suspect is? Same thing if I drag her out back, leave her in the drainage ditch. Unless… it took them a while to find her! I could cover her up with some junk; give her a chance to decompose. By the time the smell attracts attention there won't be anything to test right? Okay yeah, I admit, it's a horrible fucking idea. But my only other options- sending her to sleep with the fishes or feeding her to a herd of pigs- seem a little complicated and, well shit, impossible for someone like me who did not grow up in the mafia. I've never even committed a real crime before! (Not counting traffic infractions and casual drug use of course.)

Here goes nothing. I grab her by the feet and pull her back behind the bar and out the back door. It is pitch black outside. Charlie doesn't like to pay for any extra electricity so lucky for me there aren't any lights out here. It's about ten yards to the ditch. When we get there I feel sick to my stomach as I push Celia over the edge and she rolls to the bottom, landing in a puddle of muck with a wet thud.

The ditch is hidden by arborvitaes and another building so that it is almost invisible. I run back to the bar and grab some cardboard boxes and an old banner from the trash. This is going to work. It has to.

Dive Bar Blues Tales
FlashFiction by Riya Anne Polcastro

Detective Lin

Charlie is sweating and swearing when I walk in, muttering under his breath. "Can't... fuck... stupid pigs." He has an unlit cigarette between his lips, worn and wilted around the edges of the filter. He doesn't look at me, just the floor, and he is gone before I have put my stuff away.

Not GONE gone. His car is still in the parking lot. He is still here somewhere. Maybe he is in the back room, or in his cave Detective's Badge and IDof an office. Whatever. Either way, he is gone but he is here. It happens like that sometimes. He's still here but he's disappeared. When he reappears, it will be on the sly. He is quite stealthy for an overweight middle aged man.

There is a business card on the bar, next to the event log which is open and my entry from three nights ago is underlined in red. No issues, Tina. The card is white with blue lettering and a gold facsimile of a badge. Detective John Lin it reads. Keizer Police Department, Missing Persons it says.

My heart races. My hands shake as I pick it up. Turn it over. The name Celia Perez is scrawled across the back. I think I am going to throw up.

Then Charlie is there. I didn't hear him walk up. Didn't know he was there until he spoke, "He wants the tape from a few nights ago." He nods at the card in my hand.

The color has drained from my face, I am sure, and I am afraid he can see the panic in it instead. I take a deep breath and try to compose myself.

But Charlie doesn't notice. He is too flustered. "He said if I don't give it to him he's going to investigate me on conspiracy charges. Says he thinks I'm covering for someone." He crosses his arms over his chest and sighs loudly. Everyone knew he had done it in the past… "But the thing is it really is gone." It really is. Destroyed forever. No one would ever find it. I made sure. I cringe at the thought of my boss taking the fall. I cringe again after what he says next. "That detective might be back. He said he would be back for the tape around seven." Charlie shrugs. "I don't know what to do, I've got to leave and it's nowhere to be found."

"Wh wh wh," I stutter. "What should I tell the detective?" My heart pounds in my chest.

"The hell if I know…" and he throws his hands in the air and walks out, leaving me to figure out what to say.

I know it's him the second he walks through the door in his untailored two for one clearance Men's Warehouse polyester blend suit. He is short and squat but he still commands the room, still scares the shit out of me. He introduces himself and I explain about Charlie not being able to find the tape. He huffs and rolls his eyes, "Yeah I figured so much." He pulls a notepad and pen from the pocket inside his cheap suit. "Do you mind answering some questions?"

I choke back my alarm and try to nod, try not to look suspicious. His black eyes bore into me, just like my father's used to when I would tell him I was going to the library but really it was football games and house parties. He asks me my name and if I was working that night. He asks me if I saw Celia. It's trap. He knows she was here. I'm not the first person he has talked to and there's an electric record, seeing as how she used the ATM. "She was here, yeah. I don't understand. What is this all about?" I lie. "Did something happen to her?"

"She never made it home," he says. "Did you see her leave with anyone?"

I shake my head no. Keep it simple. She left. I don't know anything.

"Was there anyone suspicious hanging around the bar? Anyone that could have followed her?"

Again, shake my head no.

"Was she drunk when she left?"

No, she was dead. I say to myself. This guy must think I am stupid, why would I convict myself of over serving?

"Her friends seem to think maybe her ex is involved. Did you see a…" he flips through his notes and then reads a name, "Ramon Guitierrez?"

I shake my head, "I don't know who that is."

The detective finally gives up, hands me his card, and says, "Tell your boss I'm losing patience. He better come up with that tape by this time tomorrow or else."

Dive Bar Blues Tales
FlashFiction by Riya Anne Polcastro

Spiked, Part Three

Friday night- time to put the Visine, the body in the ditch, Detective Lin, all of it, out of my head and make some money. The music is up, the beer is flowing, the shots are being tossed back. The regulars are here to belt their hearts out on karaoke. Crack heads and immigrants crowd the lottery machines. Leeches look for a mark, the perfect place to stand when drinks are bought in rounds. There are even some new faces in the crowd: a few tanning bed blonds are crowded around the bar, sipping on Cosmos while their two-sizes-too-small-mixed-martial-arts-t shirt-wearing-boyfriends take turns on the punching bag machine (also known as the dick measuring stick).

Everything is going great. Sales are good. The dollars in my tip jar are piling up. The atmosphere is chill; none of the usual psychos have shown their faces. I'm carrying a tray of drinks to a table when the room goes cold and I feel the weight slip from my fingers.

I see a ghost. Celia's ghost. At the table, waiting for her vodka cran just like the rest of the girls. They laugh and joke and she flips her hair and smiles right at me, just in time to watch me drop the tray with hers and everyone else's drinks on it. "Oh Tina, when did you get so clumsy?"

"How?" I stutter. "Where?"… "How? I thought you were dead?" She was dead. She didn't have a pulse. I drug her out to the ditch. "There was a detective here." My words are slow, cautious. My hands shake as I kneel down to pick up the mess. Everyone is staring. "He said you were dead."

"Oh my god," she says, slamming her hands down on the table. "You're not going to believe what happened to me!" Her words grow muffled, as if she is telling me the story from underwater. "I woke up in a ditch!" She turns and points towards the back of the bar. "That ditch! The one back there. Can you believe it? I was there the whole time. Just passed the fuck out! Tina, how drunk was I that night?"

My pulse races and my lips stammer. "I…"

The girls laugh and say things in Spanish that I don't understand. "Exactly," Celia says. "How much did I drink?"

I can feel the sweat collecting on my brow, pouring out of my palms. What should I say?

"The last thing I remember is sitting at the bar, talking to you…"

"You shouldn'ta server her that much," a girl who forgot to draw her eyebrows on says. "That's irresponsible."

"Yeah," another girl agrees. "Couldn't you lose your license?"

"I…I.." I stammer again.

"Psssccchhh, chill out," Celia laughs. "Not like I died. And I woulda been pissed if she had cut me off!"

But you did die! You were totally dead! "How… how…" There is so much glass on the floor I give up and stand. I'm going to need a broom and a dustpan. Charlie is going to be pissed. He'll probably try to charge me for the broken glasses. But she was dead!

"How did I pass out in a ditch for like four days?" I can't seem to say anything so I just nod. She shrugs. "I guess I was just that tired."

Sucky Sucky, Part Two

Susanne stares at the empty poster board, twirling the huge black marker between her fingers. In her head she runs through all of the different slogans she has carried since she was old enough to hold a sign. There were the classics: *abortion is murder* and *abortion stops a beating heart*. And the more recent: *I am the pro-choice generation*. Her mother still has a Polaroid of her from her first Right to Life rally taped to the fridge. Just nine months old, her sign read *My mom chose life!* If you look at the photo close enough you can see the rubber bands that kept it in her chubby little hands. Obviously, that slogan won't do. None of the originals will. She taps the pen against the poster, deep in thought but her mind is as blank as the board.

What she needs is something new. Something that fits the new situation. Something that will nip the shift in popular opinion in the bud.

She can feel her pulse start to race as her thoughts wander back to church this past Sunday. The preacher's words echo from his rant at the pulpit to her ears now, "Times have changed." She can feel the hair stand up on the back of her neck and down her arms all over again. She still can't believe it. What had changed? A life is still a life is still a life! No matter who is carrying it!

Susanne frowns. She yanks the lid off of the marker and presses the pen to the poster board. She starts to write. When she is done she smiles.

Just a few hundred miles away three young women stare at a computer screen in disbelief. The first girl, Frita, tells the second to play it again. Jess clicks on the news clip front and center on the screen and the blond woman in the frame is brought back to life. "Across the nation churches and religious organizations have been changing their position on abortion almost overnight." The woman keeps talking even as she is replaced by screenshots of press releases from churches big and small. "From Catholics to Evangelicals, Christians everywhere are singing a new, pro-choice tune." The press releases continue to shuffle across the screen as the reporter lists off the pro-life organizations and crisis pregnancy centers that have closed their doors over the past six weeks. The shot cuts to the United States senate next, where members are in the middle of a historic vote to legalize abortion in all its forms, from conception right up until birth.

The third young woman feels her heart drop into her stomach all over again. Everything she wants to say gets choked up in the back of her throat. Arms crossed over her chest, she turns away from the computer and heads for the front door. The other women call after her. "Sasha, what's wrong? Sasha!"

Without a word, without so much as a glance over her shoulder, she lets the door slam behind her. The tears start in a steady stream down Sasha's face as she breaks into a run. When she reaches the elevator she holds her breath and punches the button. She squeezes her eyes shut while she waits but it's too much, she can't hold it in. The stairs are at the other end of the hall, the fire door just a short sprint away. The stairwell is empty. There is no one to witness the salty moisture on her face or complain about how her sobs echo off of the cement walls. She races down flight after flight of stairs, her footfalls echoing along with her cries, her vision blurry from so many tears. Instead of steps she sees flashes of memory. Travelling down the fifth floor, she sees her mother in a burst of white, holding a little stick with a pink plus sign, a toothy smile stretched across her face. Down the fourth floor she watches her mother's belly grow. Down the third there's a grainy ultrasound and tears. Down the second and her mother stands in front of the congregation, her abdomen swollen near eight months. She smiles, a mask for her fear, as the preacher praises her choice to put her unborn child's life before her own. She can still hear him, the arrogance in his voice as he advertises her martyrdom, sets her up as an example among women. Down the first floor and there is blood — blood and her mother's eyes, already glassy, the light gone long before they found her cold on the kitchen floor.

Over on the west coast, Marcus' heart races and his palms sweat while he waits for the doctor to return. His voice catches in his throat when two raps finally fall against the double wide door. Even without his response, the door swings open and a man in a long white coat with a wispy comb over enters. "Private Dunaway?" he asks.

Marcus nods, his forehead wrinkled, base terror in his eyes. He doesn't ask. He doesn't have to. He can see it in the doctor's eyes.

Still, the old man takes his time, works his way up to the bad news. "So," he says as he sits down on a swivel stool. He scoots and then slides a few feet across the shiny white floor so that he is face to face with his patient. "You recently spent some time on Tinurtia?" The young soldier nods. He clenches his jaw, tries to hide his fear, but the grimace under his skin shines through anyway. The old man drops the soldier's chart on the counter beside him. He sighs one long, exaggerated sigh. "I don't think I really need to tell you what's going on." He pauses and Marcus hangs his head. "You watch the news," he snorts. "Not to mention most of the guys you came back with are already. . ."

A life is a life no matter who is pregnant. Back in the Bible Belt Susanne draws two symbols — one in pink with a circle and a cross below it, another in blue with what looks almost like an arrow pointing away from a second circle —

under the word pregnant. When she is done she leans back on her heels and admires her work. Hands on her hips, she smiles. To herself she says, "Can't argue with that."

Back on the other side of the country, Marcus tries to anyway. "But Doc. It's not possible!"

The old doctor shakes his head. His white hair flops around. "You think I don't know that? Of course men can't get pregnant! It goes against everything we've ever known about the human body!" Marcus' face goes red from frustration. He demands to know how this happened to him, how it happened to half the guys in his platoon. The doctor crosses his arms over his chest and leans back against the counter. "You're the one who had sex with a Tinurtian, you tell me!"

It is only a matter of time before the more sensational of television networks is explaining it to anyone who will watch, complete with artistic renditions and digital re-enactments. On one particular channel, already well known for its anchor panel of blonde bimbos eager to obsess over and trash all non-traditional sex, viewers are given a CGI close up of a Tinurtian's vagina while one of their pseudo-scientists describes it in detail in the voice over. Susanne watches in shock as the science-y sounding voice describes how, when the human male inserts his phallus into the suction cup in the Tinutian female's crotch, his seed is sucked out and mixed with an egg that she excretes into said suction cup. In an instant fertilization takes place and the female shoots the fertilized egg back up the human male's urethra, impregnating him. Susanne reminds the television that life begins at conception but even the most conservative of conservatives appear to have flip flopped, betrayed their sacred Christian vows to protect the sanctity of life, and sold out to the abortion industry.

She grabs the remote, surfs the channels until the TV lands on that old standby — that beacon for pro-life

fundamentalism — the 700 Club. If anyone is still sane, she
assures herself, it is the voice of reason.

Pat Robertson. Sasha still sees him in her nightmares.
She still wakes up screaming in the middle of the night.
His goat like eyes, his thin sinister lips, they still haunt her
nightmares. Trapped in sleep, he reads to her. He reads
the letter her mother wrote to him just after the
ultrasound. It echoes between her ears, and so does his
response. "It's the devil testing you." Neckless, bodyless,
just his talking head swirls behind her sleeping eyes. He
tells her mother the abortion industry will do anything to
turn a profit, anything to kill babies. "Your baby won't kill
you," he warbles. "But your sin will." There was still hope
when Sasha's mother wrote the letter. With his response,
Mr. Pat Robertson tore that hope to shreds along with any
chance that her mother would save her own life. At that
point she was just a vessel, something that meant less than
the near dead fetus inside of her.

Luckily for Marcus, and all of his fellow soldiers who
got a little space booty, that kind of thinking doesn't apply
to Y chromosomes. Reproductive rights make a complete
one eighty when the all-male Discovery crew comes back
all-pregnant. Those drive-thru abortion clinics the
feminists used to joke would pop u on every street corner
if men could get pregnant, they become a reality. Well at
least the one on base does anyway and there is line around
the block before it even opens for its first day of business.

From the safety of his Jeep, Private Dunaway taps the
steering wheel nervously. He bounces one knee, then the
other. He tosses his head back and runs his fingers
through his hair. He sucks in one deep breath after
another, forgetting to exhale. As he gets closer to the front
of the line someone catches his eye. A lone protestor, her
hair is long and stringy, her clothes are dirty, and there are
bags under her eyes. She waves a tattered sign with pink
and blue symbols that looks like it travelled a thousand
miles, if not more, to admonish him for his choice.

His anger is instant. Who is she to tell him that he has to carry this thing to term? Who the fuck is she to tell him what to do with his body?

Susanne sees him frowning at her, staring her down, so she does what she was always taught to do. She smiles right at him, eye to eye, and yells, "God loves you!" She reminds herself to stay strong, she is a soldier in God's army, and even if she is the very last one she will fight to the end. She will fight to save those innocent lives! She moves a few feet closer, to the edge of the buffer zone, and peers into his eyes. Then she yells, "God loves your baby!"

Marcus wants to tell her it's not a baby and call her a crazy bitch but the line is moving. It's almost his turn. The closer he gets the longer each patient in front of him seems to take. From the sidewalk, the protestor implores him with her big wet eyes. His gut rocks and sways and he reaches for the barf bag on the passenger seat. He is sick and angry and confused all at the same time.

The van in front of him pulls away, a giddy squeal in its rear tires. Marcus takes a deep breath and eases the Jeep forward. He stops on the side of the building, next to an open doorway. There is a stool in the doorway, one of those swiveling doctor stools, and that is all. He shuts off the engine and waits with baited breath. A moment later an old woman appears in the doorway. She has to be at least sixty and she is pulling latex gloves on over hands and sitting down on the stool. She smiles and tells him to drop his pants. "This is going to hurt," she says, just as the door behind her swings open. A young woman in all black stands in the doorway. She raises something black and double barreled. Gripping it with both hands, she squeezes the trigger.

"This is for my mother!" Sasha cries, mascara run down her face. Boom! Boom! Pieces of the doctor splatter around the white room, on Marcus' Jeep, and his baby bump. She lowers the gun to reload and catches the pregnant man in her sight. She spits, "Murderer."

The Truth about Cows

Nana always warned me not to underestimate the milk sows but Grand Pap said not to mind her. Said she was a bit loopy ever since she ran the combine into the barn after one too many half glasses of red blend. Still, when I was little I used to sit on the big flat boulder in the middle of the back field and watch them for hours. I wanted to believe Nana. So I watched and waited for one of them to surprise me. I waited and waited and waited but they never did anything out of the ordinary. For hours on end I watched as they chewed their cud or started over again ripping fresh blades of grass from the earth. Sometimes they just stopped and stood there, napping on their feet. The cows were mostly silent. They didn't moo to each other in conversation. Their vacant stares were fixed to one spot for up to an hour at a time. Every so often a pair of eyes would land on me—a pair of slippery black coals hidden behind long sad lashes. Nothing. They just stared. I don't know if I thought eventually one of them was going to open her mouth and talk to me or what, but every time their eyes shifted to me my heart skipped a beat and I waited for that black and white beast to amaze me.

Later I would beg Nana, "Just tell me. Please!" And Nana would smirk and part her lips with her wrinkled fingers and for just a split second I would think she was going to spill the beans and tell me the truth about cows, but she never did. Instead, she'd bite her lips in half smile and repeat the same reminder—never underestimate the milk sows.

Grand Pap caught me out there on that rock more

times than I could count. Most times he'd laugh at me, tell me I was wasting my time and to get back to my homework. Until one time he was in a foul, sarcastic mood. He snapped at me. "Why would they do anything with you staring at them like that? You'd be better off hiding in them bushes." He didn't mean it, he was just sick of finding me out in the field acting like a milk sow myself (the hours of nothing, not the cud chewing—just to be clear). But I didn't care. At the time I thought his snarky words were brilliant! The next day when I went out to watch the cows I hid in the bushes just like Gran Pap suggested. And I waited.

They still didn't do anything.

But the day after that they did. Well, one of them did. And she did it before I got there so I didn't exactly witness it. When I reached the kine she was already standing on the big flat rock in the middle of the field. I still have no idea how she got up there. Or how she got back down. She just stood there, staring at me with her eyes like big black holes, and I stood there staring back at her until the hair on my arms stood on end. A crow screamed in the distance and I backed away, out of the field. I didn't turn around until I had the farmhouse in my sights. That night when Nana reminded me the blood went cold in my veins.

That was the last time I went out to that field. Until today. Until Nana went missing.

I was sure she would be there! So sure!

Never underestimate the milk sows.

I climbed onto the flat rock where the Holstein had stood the last time I was here. I stood on it like she had and looked around at the field. Nana wasn't there. So I waited and waited—just like I did as a kid. My legs grew weary so I sat. The sky grew dark so laid down. I don't know when I fell asleep but I woke to Nana's giant head in the sky.

Never underestimate the milk sows.

I closed my eyes, took a deep breath, and let it out

slow. The next time I woke it was morning and the cows were gone. I stood and jumped off the boulder, dusted myself off. I needed coffee—black coffee and a cigarette.

There's a diner downtown where my friend is a regular. Any day of the week I can find him there from eight to three, at the last sidewalk table, a bottomless cup of coffee and a half full ashtray pushed to the edge of the table to make room for his laptop. This time he had half a glazed doughnut on his lap and crumbs on his keyboard. I sat across from him but he didn't so much as acknowledge me.

"Hi."

His eyes darted back and forth across the screen. He croaked, "Hi."

"I still don't know the truth about cows."

"I know," he says without looking up.

I sighed in defeat. That is when a hooligan in a black leather jacket sprinted past us followed by an old woman in house shoes and a duster. I knew that duster! "Nana!"

I took off after them. I called after my Nana but she ignored me. She kept chasing him without looking back at me once. Half-way down the block the hooligan ran out of breath. Nana caught up with him in just a few strides. She grabbed him by him collar and shouted in his face, "I said give me your wallet you fucking punk!"

$17

A week or so after Rose is taken in, there is a knock at the door, and my heart sinks as I imagine the police on the other side that are here to tell me that my aunt committed suicide on the ward. I answer the door relieved but confused to see a young man dressed from head to toe in red instead. He pauses for a second, bows his cornrowed head, and then stumbles in practiced measure, "Is Jessica home?"

I furrow my brow and respond that he has the wrong place. He is nervous and shifts from one foot to the other.

"Did Jessica used to live here?"

I shake my head, "Not that I know of."

There is something peculiar about him. He is thugged out but more rap video than real-life thug, complete with high-end kicks and freshly pressed designer jeans. His dewy brown skin is flawless, even impeccable—so much so that it should contradict his next question. "Hey, I don't mean to bother you, but do you do crystal?" He hops from his left foot to his right; his nerves creep and crawl across his face. "A honey like you, I'll hook you up fat."

I stare back at him blankly. Is that a skinny joke? Or is he actually stupid enough to be going door-to-door to sell meth with his Jessica story? There is something very odd going on here, and it calls to me to explore where the trail leads. Crazy? Maybe. Maybe I need a little bit of crazy in my life; maybe I am not only used to it, maybe I like it. With my aunt on a psych hold, this situation presents the opportunity to furnish it myself.

"No, I don't do crystal." I say, the insult heavy in my

voice. "Got any coke instead?" I offer him seventeen dollars and a five-dollar bud.

He tells me he does not, but he should be able to hook it up if he can get a ride. Now, perhaps this is where I should close the door, but my instincts do not tell me to. Fear does not come knocking right behind him. He could be an undercover cop (although an awfully nervous one). Or a carjacker. Or murderer/rapist.

But none of these thoughts so much as cross my mind. What does is that Angela and I have a date at the strip club tonight, and she is all out of booger sugar. Furthermore, this cat smells like fear himself, and in this small exchange, I have already established a position of power at the cellular level. My mind has taken on a different level. More and more so as of late. A whole new element of existence is exposed. This is not a state of invincibility, a typical drug-induced state, but rather one in which I simply do not give a fuck. Maybe every move cannot be anticipated, but I am confident enough in my understanding of the situation to maintain control. Most importantly, no matter how hard he tries to imagine it, when he looks at me, he does not see a very good victim for whatever his motives are. Sweat has already started to form on his brow as he climbs into the passenger seat of my car.

On his direction, we head over to 25th Street by the post office. This is the part of Felony Flats with literal box-like flats. Most of the people desperate enough to reside in these shacks are sex offenders and homicide parolees. There are also plenty of older, semi-rundown houses lining the street, and I pull over when he points towards a group of people hanging out on the front porch.

"I need the money," he says.

"You want the pot too?"

"Nah, they'll just hook up a short sack."

He takes the cash and walks over to talk to someone on the porch. They chat for quite a while, and there are shrubs between them and my car, so I cannot tell if anything is exchanged. When he comes back, he tells me he did not have any luck, but he is pretty sure that his other homeboy will be able to help us out; we just need to go down the street a little further.

This time, he has me park in a visitor's spot in an apartment complex, and I wait in the car while he walks up the stairs and disappears from view again. He is gone even longer this time, and my annoyances stack one right on top of another. It is getting late, and I was planning to hit the gym before it is time to go out. I had just changed into my workout clothes before this oddball knocked on my door, and now I'm freezing in my booty shorts and wifebeater.

Not that I am not used to the quest. Sometimes it takes a few contacts before you score. But this does not feel right; he is up to something, but it cannot possibly be worth a mere seventeen dollars. I cannot imagine what kind of con he could be running here unless it is simply to play chauffeur for his Jessica meth gig. Still, my curiosity is stronger than my desire for cardio, so it is a conscious decision to see where this game will lead. It is no big surprise when he comes back empty-handed again. At this point, my strategy is to sit back and watch him play himself out. At worst, I will be out seventeen dollars, but it will be worth it to watch him really sweat.

After a third stop and still nothing, he asks me to stop at a store. Suspicious, I follow him inside for a soda. He selects something out of the glass case behind the counter where the pipes and tooters are. Back in the car, he says, "I have one more hookup to check."

My senses are a little too heightened right now, so I say, "That's fine, but I'm going home to smoke a bowl first." A couple of hits should calm them down. Back at the cottage, I decide to roll a joint to smoke while we drive instead. Without asking, he grabs a CD case off of a shelf then reaches into his jacket and pulls a small baggie from an inside pocket. Inside is not cocaine. It is all rocks—more translucent than white. Crystal. He takes a razor blade from his pocket and chops it up. As rampant as the stuff is in the Willamette Valley, I have seen it on only a few occasions and never ever chopped up. Smoked, yes. Shot-up, OK. But chopped up? Um, no. Not that I have ever been interested enough to pay it any attention. Meth is a dirty drug cooked up in bathtubs by street chemists that convinces its users to turn away from grooming and personal hygiene and steal everything in sight. And now here is some well-dressed tweaker chopping it up in my living room and asking me if I would like a line.

He bought that shit with my money. He was never trying to hook up any cocaine nor did he have any meth to sell to begin with. This fucker was soliciting to be a go-between, not just so that he could skim a little off the top, but so he could make off with the entire sack. I was not in search of the right cure for his craving, so he lied some more, and now he is putting my seventeen dollars up his nose right in front of me.

He is done before I finish rolling the joint. "Can I borrow your phone?"

I nod and he goes outside to make a call. When he comes back, he sits next to me on the couch. He still has my phone open, and it looks like he is playing with the camera. Then he goes and tries to nudge my knees apart like he is going to take a crotch shot, and I snatch the phone out of his hand, burning through his pupils with my own. "Don't fucking touch me."

He shrinks back from my rage and off of the couch. It is not clear whether he was testing my inhibitions or my fight, but he will not try either again.

When I have finished rolling the joint, we leave to check with his last fictional hookup, this time parking on a quiet street in the suburbs. And once again, I wait in the car while he walks down a few houses and disappears from view. He has me on a wild goose chase. But does he really think I will drive him to so many places that I will forget I gave him my money in the first place?

Once more, he returns without anything — just as expected. "But I just remembered another homie . . ."

"Nah," I interrupt, flipping a U-turn back to my house. "How about you just give me money back instead?"

He shoots me a quick look like a child caught with his hand in the cookie jar and then starts digging in his pockets furiously. "Oh, oh shit," he lies. "I must have dropped it."

Calm and quiet, I just watch him fumble as he cooks up his story. I do not understand his nervousness. What does he have to fear? I am a buck twenty-five and unarmed as far as he knows. He is almost twice my size; what does he possibly think I am going to do to him? Why doesn't he just admit that he stole my money, say "sorry bitch," and get out of my car? What does he think I am going to do about it? Chase him through suburban backyards and camouflaged trailer parks? He has the look of someone who has taken on more than he can handle and is pissing his pants trying to get out of it when he blunders, "I must've dropped it. Yeah, I must've dropped it in front of my homegirl Sandy's house."

"Well, then let's go back and get it," I say dryly, wondering how long he will try to keep up this charade.

"See, she's not home anymore, so we'll have to go see her at work. I'm sure she picked it up."

At this point, my only plan is to go with the flow and trust that an opportunity will present itself. This supposed homegirl works at the adult shop down the road. I follow him inside, and he wanders around, ducking in and out of rows of dildos and pocket pussies as if he is trying to get lost among them while trying to appear as though he is looking for someone. When he does not find who he is not looking for, we leave the store empty-handed, and he doesn't say a word to the solitary clerk.

"Um, she must not be here yet. We're gonna have to

wait."

So we go back to my car, and he is restless and fidgety for a few short moments before it all gets to be too much for him, and he heads back inside, claiming he needs to use the phone. I watch him go inside through my rearview mirror and dial Daemon. Julia answers with suspicion instead. I ask to speak to her boyfriend and ask him what my best move would be.

"Are you asking me to come down there and help you out?"

"Nah," I answer. "Not exactly. I'm not sure that seventeen dollars is worth taking it to that level. It's more just the principle of the matter, you know? I just want to know what you think I should do in this kind of situation."

"Where you at?" he asks.

"The porn shop on Lancaster. You really don't need to come down here; I was just hoping for some advice."

"We're just down the street."

In my rearview mirror, I see the front door of the porn shop open, and this nervous tweaker hustler walks back out towards my car. For all he knows, I do not even see him. I'm just a dumb white girl talking on her cell phone, not paying attention to anything or anyone else. Or so he thought when he knocked on my door. Why doesn't he just walk away now? I get out and meet him beside my car. Daemon wants to know what he is claiming.

"Bloods," he answers, as if that is the end all be all of it.

I roll my eyes at the obvious. "More specific . . ." He responds with something completely nonsensical. "Las Vegas Pimps?" He nods and I have to choke back my laughter. On the phone, Daemon laughs as well. "Hey, let him know he's in Westside territory. Whatever little crew he ran with down there in the desert don't mean shit here. Tell him I'm on my way to come talk to him."

I do and Pimp here nods. "OK, OK." He takes a pair of white leather gloves out of his pocket. They are fingerless with Velcro straps.

"He's putting on his fighting gloves," I tell Daemon. We both laugh.

After we hang up, he tells me that he is going to wait inside. He is nervous but not nervous enough; yet another chance to escape and he passes it up. Maybe it is the shit he snorted. Maybe he thinks there are no real gangsters in Salem, Oregon and gravely underestimates his predicament.

I stand outside my car and watch the door. Daemon and Julia arrive in no time. We all go in together and walk through the entire store, down the same rows of videos and dildos all over again; we even look inside the arcades. They are waiting for me to point him out, staring at me like I failed to notice that he had gotten away. We circle around to the front of the store and notice that there is a restroom. The lock reads "unoccupied," but there is an obvious presence behind the door. We look at each other, back at the door, and back at each other. The lock slides quietly over to "occupied."

At this point, the clerk has picked up on the tension and eyes us for a moment before reaching for the phone. She dials a very short number and continues to stare at us while she talks.

"I think she's calling the police," Julia says.

"We should leave," Daemon agrees.

In the parking lot, I thank them for their help, and Julia hugs me good-bye. While she waits to turn out of the parking lot, the Vegas Pimp ducks out of the shop and darts across the street right in front of her. She rolls her window down and yells back at me, "That him?"

But of course it is not worth chasing a tweaker across five lanes of traffic. Daemon runs into him again a few weeks later. Cat gets one look and takes off running again. Daemon gives chase just for fun, but as they say, "You ain't catching no crackhead." And that one is still running over seventeen dollars.

$17 is an excerpt from the novel Jane. by Riya Anne Polcastro.

The remaining stories in this section came from the development of Teeth, the namesake character for the working title of Riya Anne Polcastro's upcoming horror/noir crime novel which she is hoping to (finally!) have out somewhere around the beginning of 2016.

The Anger

It is an anger deep and primal. It snarls and growls and wants to tear at your flesh slow, with determination, with purpose. It hungers for the chance, thirsts to tear you limb from limb. It doesn't fear you. No matter what you wanted to do first, no matter your intentions. It will find you. Stalk you. Eat you alive. It shakes with anticipation when it feels your presence. Its lips curl. Rabid saliva collects at the corners of its mouth.

It is true, I have nurtured it. I have fed it in my darkest hours, stoked its appetite. And it is hungry now. Voracious. Indomitable. I am almost afraid of it, afraid of myself. Afraid of what I might do. Afraid of what I am capable of. But my hate is stronger than my fear. And even though I don't know you, I hate you and I want to hurt you. Hurt you in a way you could never imagine, a way you could never recover from. Hurt you in a way that burrows into your brain; chews on your cerebellum. Nibbles on your hippocampus. All thoughts, conscious, unconscious, all of them, they will come from me; doused and flooded with the haunted corpse of my rage.

I work late at night. Welding and cutting. My eyes strain and grow tired in the lamplight. But the anger inside pushes me on.

This is my third design. The springs were wound too tight on the first. There was a good chance I would injure myself. The second was too flimsy. It would trap the target, true. But it would not sever it. This one, this one will be perfect. I can feel it.

This is not something that can be rushed; patience is

imperative. But rage does not know patience. It must be given acquiescence. So it crouches, watches for opportunity, learns to recognize it, makes a plan, writes a script and practices it. There is little room to fear what could go wrong. The animal inside of me is taking over and I am confident that it will prevail. It isn't just angry, it is vengeful in its hunger. When it is in charge, my mouth waters at the thought of your flesh: young, tender, virgin so far as my purposes are concerned.

"I've been waiting for you," it will say.

And when the razors that are its teeth, when they grip your flesh, when they tear your member from its roots, when the laugh, too deep and curdled, too masculine for its voluptuous lips, when all of that happens, what are you going to do then? Suffer. Alone. Cold and bleeding out. Ashamed and desperate. Like the justice that has just been served to you, golden platter and all.

Sometimes I have to stop working because the laughter shakes my belly. It gives me too much joy, too much gratification; the thought of you lying in the alley, the perpetrator now the victim.

A man like you is easy to mark. You wear your intentions in your walk, in your stare, in your approach. A man like you never thinks the better can be gotten of him. He never thinks it could be a trap.

A man like you isn't a man at all.

A man like you must be taught a lesson.

My blood pressure rises and my hands shake with anticipation as adrenaline rushes though my system. I put my tools down. Time for a break.

I climb the stairs out of my basement apartment and go through the door at the top into the utility room. The kitchen is just off of the utility room, past the washer and dryer. Katrina, my roommate, is at the table, looking over her kids' homework. "How are you?" she asks as I grab a glass from the cupboard and the lemonade from the fridge. "You've been cooped up all evening. What are you doing down there?"

I pour the lemonade and shrug as I put the pitcher back in the refrigerator. "I like being alone sometimes. Don't take it personally." I carry my glass to the table and set it down across from her. "I've just been knitting, nothing to worry about. Nothing weird." A smirk tugs at the corner of my lip but I force it down. If only she knew.

"As long as you're not writing suicide notes or anything…"

"I am definitely not writing suicide notes!" I assure her.

"Good, good," she says, absentminded as she scans over the homework in front of her. "But you seem a little…" she looks back up, "frazzled? Are you sure you don't need some vodka in that lemonade?"

I smile and shake my head, do my best to be convincing and not blush. "What? No. I'm fine. Great, actually." I pause, for effect. "Really? Do you really think I look frazzled?"

Katrina looks back up from the papers on the table. "It's probably just me. Sorry. I must be… what's that called? Deflecting?" She sighs. "This is really hard." She leans back in her chair and throws her hands up in the air. "I'm stumped by ninth grade geometry. What am I going to do when he gets to calculus, trigonometry?"

What would she do if she knew what I was building in her basement? My cheeks start to flush but I fight back against it.

We talk about her struggles as a single parent, my job, her job, the sub development planned for down the street. I finish my lemonade and head back down the narrow basement stairs. Instead of going back to work, I decide not to rush it. I grab the brush from my nightstand and stroke it gently through each and every lock of my hair. Next, I floss, and brush my teeth, put on pajamas, and climb into bed. My project is a blur in the distance as I turn out the lamp on the nightstand. I smile to myself and drift off to sleep. The time would come. Soon. Very soon.

Scar Tissue

Showers are the worst. Showers remind him of everything.

He stitched the wound himself with nothing more than a needle and thread. It was not the sort of thing he could have gone to the hospital for. It wasn't the sort of crime he could have explained away. Twenty three years seven months and sixteen days later he still wakes up screaming. He still wakes up screaming and searching and grasping for something that is never there. Then he cries, laments his regrets like a spoiled toddler.

It still is not his fault. No. That bitch had no right. No right whatsoever.

On the rare occasion that he ventures out, he still watches for her, still sees her blond hair in the crowd. She has not aged a year, or even a day, no, not a single solitary moment. Her bubbly green eyes follow him; her freckled nose still crinkles with the same innocence and naïveté that had made her the perfect mark.

Except that she wasn't, she was not the real mark at all. He was. Trickster bitch! She sucked him in. Twenty three years seven months and sixteen days ago. It was not his fault. She took advantage of him, of his wants, his desires, his needs. His right to take what he wants! And now? Now he is the one that lives as a hermit, he is the one afraid to enter public washrooms with their rows of urinals, their rows of penises on display. What is he to do? Use a stall? Tinkle like a lass into a porcelain pond? He is the one that cowers in his mobile home while she stalks the streets for fresh meat.

He does blind spit baths in the dark; changes his bottoms only when he has confused the rumble in his tummy for mere gas; and, really it goes without saying, never ever masturbates. In fact, everything he does, he does in a manner of avoidance; anything to keep from looking at it; anything NOT to look it in the eye. But in the shower… in the shower it is too hard to look away. It calls to him with a siren song of torment. It says her name.

Teeth… Teeth…

He had heard rumors of course. Rumors about a woman on the hunt for men like him. He had laughed it off as an urban legend, a story recycled through the ages, it couldn't possibly be true. A silly myth was not going to stop him.

Except it wasn't a myth.

TEETH!

He stares at the ceiling, the curtain rod, the soap dish, anything but the gnarled flesh that hisses up at him through the drone of the shower head. He looks past it, to the months of filth that wash down the drain.

Teeeeeeeeeth……

He scrunches his eyes closed; shakes his head; pounds his fists against his temples. And when he cannot take it anymore, when he cannot ignore the voice any longer, he opens his eyes and looks down. Twenty three years seven months and sixteen days with nothing but lumpy purple scar tissue, his lonely scrotum flapping in the stream of hot water.

Scar Tissue first appeared in Volume One of the Artificial Selection Project Literary Journal in March 2014.

Teeth: an intro of sorts

(Now) If she knew then what she knows now you would not have lived. If she knew then what she knows now she would have dug her thumbs into your eye sockets, through the congealed jelly of your corneas, into the gray matter of your frontal lobe. If she knew then what she knows now she would have ripped your eyelids from your face. If she knew then what she knows now she would have torn your lips from your skull with no more than her bare teeth. If she knew then what she knows now she would have shredded your skin and stripped your flesh from the bone. If she knew then what she knows now she would have twisted and pulled. If she knew then what she knows now she would have chased after you like a rabid dog. Snarling and clawing and biting thirsty for your blood.

But she knows better now.

She has Teeth.

And that is all she will ever need.

Now she does not fear she waits in anticipation. Salivating. Fantasizing. Hungry for vengeance. The monster inside of her grabs the bars of its cage and shakes her diaphragm with a knee quivering growl.

If she knew then what she knows now, she would have left its cage unlocked.

She twirls the key on her finger, at the ready. It is only a matter of time now. Its hunger quakes through her. She does not fight it. Nay she feeds it, fuels its appetite.

If she knew then what she knows now she would have woke the monster up a long time ago.

She clenches and it gnashes. Teeth. At first she was afraid. Not anymore. Now she is eager in her zealous quest. She would find him. And when she did… when they did…

(Later) These days he only left for supplies. Things like gasoline, candle wicks and powdered milk. He made do with as little as possible.

He had developed a taste for powdered milk. True, he did not like it right away; it took a while to grow on him. It was thin, with a papery consistency like baby food, almost as flavorful as cardboard. But it doesn't go bad. It doesn't curdle in the fridge. He only made as much as he would use in a day anyway. And he could buy enough for a year at the local cost club without the clerk so much as batting an eye.

(Now) She laughs. Above and below. The monster has a mind of its own. Once she lets it out will she be able to get it back in its cage? Will she be able to stop at just him?

She smirks. Does she even want to? There is so much vengeance due all over the world.

So many debts left unpaid. So much karma left to ripen for too many lifetimes. In a way it would be selfish not to give the monster its rampage.

(Later) I lied. He left to sell the garlic too. Once a year he went to a farmer's market. The garlic was his cheddar. A little under the table income the SSI people didn't know about. Organic. Lawn grown garlic. Fertilized by god knows how many neighborhood dogs. The owners always looked away. Pretended like they did not see.

What didn't sell, he ate. Grilled. Fried. Straight, like an apple. It poured from his pores, covered his skin with a layer of allium. It was the sort of rancid stank that kept people away. Even concerned neighbors waived from the sidewalk. They would hardly come in to say hello, confront his earthy layers up close.

(Now) Teeth wants to maim first. If murder is a natural consequence then so be it. It is only fair. It is how They operate. It is what They do.

She stalks the night in search of him. Like an animal she sniffs at the air in hopes of catching his scent. She pretends not to look down dark alleys and behind dumpsters. She hides her intentions behind the façade of an easy victim, defenseless and out too late. She shutters in anticipation. The key is in the lock. All she has to do is turn it and the monster will be loose.

(Later) Of all of the victims, he was the only one to survive. It was what led him to live as a recluse, a hermit; the weird guy with the heavy beard that grew a lawn full of garlic.

Dive Bar Blues Tales
FlashFiction by Riya Anne Polcastro

Night Stalker Do-Over

Closing time and I'm cleaning off the tables when I find a pile of cocktail napkins scrawled in rage soaked ink on one of the tables. The print starts out neat enough, almost like a bubbly love letter written in typical girly handwriting. But soon it decompensates into something rough that burrows through the layers of napkin, rips and tears at the dried tree pulp. I think back on who could have written it. What oddballs have been in the bar tonight? Next to the napkins there is an empty martini glass. It was an appletini, the cherry stem picked clean and left at the bottom. The only appletinis I've sold tonight went to a pudgy blue eyed blond with freckles on her nose. I try to reconcile the perky twenty something with the perfect nails and perfect hair and three hundred dollar purse on her arm with the words before me but I just can't. And as I read through them the goose bumps on my arms don't know whether to freak out and call the cops or cheer.

Dearest Richard,

I have dreamed of you for so long. Crazy intense dreams! All the stuff I want to do to you AAAAAhhhhh just thinking about it I can barely contain myself!

Those Mick Jagger cheekbones ooooh yeah, best handlebars I've ever seen! You wouldn't mind if my acrylics dug into them a little would you? I need something substantial to sink them into, something to give me extra leverage when I plunge my favorite strap on up your ass. Oh and those lips! Those lips! They're so pretty! And they are going to look fanfuckingtastic wrapped around that big fat dildo of mine. You'll make sure to lick it nice and clean for me won't you? But fuck my luck it is too late. Your dumb ass went and died before I got my chance. Death at my hands would have been so much sweeter babe! Why didn't you wait for me? Natural causes, are you kidding me? Surely the pool stick I had set aside to finish you off with would have been way more fun than the infected anal fissure you really died from. Fuck those prison guards for not saving me a piece. And I had such a great recipe for roasted dick I was going to feed you beforehand! Best. Last. Meal. Ever.

R.I.P. Richard Ramirez. Rest In hell Puto.

In honor of the Night Stalker, tonight I change my tactics. Tonight I stalk the innocent.

Maybe it's not fair to them. But it wasn't fair to your victims either Richard. And it is time the tables are turned anyway right? That part is only fair. Don't worry babe, I won't tarnish your legacy. If anything I will outshine it.

Love Always,

...

About the Author

Riya Anne Polcastro   Storyteller Grrrl.

Armed with a useless liberal arts degree, Riya Anne Polcastro is a student of human behavior and a conduit for raw words. Maybe it is because she learned to read and write in her second language before she learned to do the same in her first. Maybe it is because she was raised a missionary's daughter at the same time that she was taught to question everything. Maybe there are a whole lot of reasons. Either way, her fascination with mental illness and human interaction is weaved into fiction with a language that is at times caressed and loved, at others beaten into submission.

A longtime resident of the Pacific Northwest, Polcastro aims to join the ranks of great Oregon writers. Her first love is dark, edgy literary fiction but she also dabbles in young adult dystopia and non-fiction. While she has been heavily inspired by the genius of writers such as

Palahniuk and Tolstoy, music has also played a huge role, with artists like Gnarles Barkley and Tool having a tremendous influence in her stories.

Polcastro enjoys an active lifestyle, including running, hiking, in-line skating, and a special brand of tennis lovingly called "Get it Bitch". She also enjoys spending time with her family, making beer and getting away to British Columbia at every possible opportunity. Her favorite color is burnt orange, but it is hard to find so she wears a lot of red instead.

Visit Polcastro at www.riyaannepolcastro.com.

Proof

Made in the USA
Charleston, SC
11 October 2015